Pirate's Price

by Darlene Marshall

Pirate's Price by Darlene Marshall
ISBN 1-55316-537-3
Published by LTDBooks
www.LTDBooks.com

Previously published in electronic format by Dreams Unlimited.

Published in Canada by LTDBooks, 200 North Service Road West, Unit 1, Suite 301, Oakville, ON L6M 2Y1

Printed and bound in Canada.

National Library of Canada Cataloguing in Publication Data

Marshall, Darlene, 1955-
Pirate's price / Darlene Marshall.

Also available in electronic format.
ISBN 1-55316-537-3

I. Title.

PS3613.A767P57 2003 813'.6 C2003-905131-5

Acknowledgments

To Diana: It seems inadequate, but the words are sincere and from my heart. Thank you.

Thanks also to: Sensei Raphi and Micah for help with the fight scenes, RWA Online, CompuServe's Sailing Forum and the Literary Forum, Alachua County Library District Reference Desk.

And finally...For Howard, who said "You can dance." All I needed was the right partner.

Prologue

The cabin hatch closed behind the pirate captain. Justin stopped testing the strength of the ropes securing him and glared at the tall, masked figure leaning one padded shoulder against the hatch. The pirate's red cravat was looking wilted, the black satin shirt and coat torn and darkened by blood.

Justin noted the damage with satisfaction. It would be the first of many penalties the cur would pay for what he'd done. Even so, a frisson of fear ran down his spine. He couldn't ignore what he'd seen abovedecks and the lewd comments from the men who'd bound him to the bunk, but he knew better than to reveal his anxiety.

"Lay one hand on me, sodomite, and there won't be a hole deep enough for you to hide in!" he snarled.

The captain's eyes crinkled at the corners. The blackguard was *smiling* behind the mask!

Captain Daniels's slow glance raked the earl's lean body, bound hand and foot to the bunk. The gaze lingered on Justin's broad shoulders, sliding down his flat belly to his firmly muscled thighs. The pirate's eyes rose back to meet the earl's and didn't look away as a slender gloved hand unwrapped the red silk scarf.

"You!" Justin gasped.

Captain Daniels smiled, a smile that wasn't reflected in the gleaming brown eyes.

"Spare me your dramatics, my lord. The only thing I want from you is a divorce."

Chapter 1

East Florida, United States Possession, 1820

"No, Marlowe, I will not hear another word about my 'blushing bride' until I've a drink in my hand!"

The door hit the library wall with a crash as Justin Stephen Charles Delerue, Fifth Earl Smithton, strode toward the cupboard where he'd seen his host stash some inferior brandy. A small smile on his face, Peter Marlowe followed his best friend. It wasn't often he got to see Justin discomforted. They'd been close since school days, when Smithton had taken exception to three older boys pushing Marlowe around and had decided to even the odds.

Smithton poured a generous serving of the brandy.

"Keep pouring," Marlowe said dryly. "You're going to need it."

Smithton scowled as he shoved a glass into his friend's hand, and Marlowe's grin broadened when he saw the green eyes narrow beneath the black curls that fell across Smithton's forehead.

Justin cursed beneath his breath. At five-and-twenty, he was too young to be entering into matrimony. His looks, title, and money ensured there were always available women, and he had no desire to tie himself to anyone at this time. But circumstances had forced him across the world to this humid hellhole of St. Augustine. He followed in the wake of his father, who'd sailed here often for Delerue Shipping when Florida was under British dominion.

This was Justin's first trip to Florida, and although he could think of a hundred places he'd rather be, most of them much cooler, he prepared for the inevitable the same way he'd learned to deal with most of his problems—see if he could turn it to his advantage and make a profit off the transaction.

His cronies sneered at his "tradesman's mentality," but he was used to ignoring other people's opinions. The Delerue family and its holdings, particularly Delerue Shipping, were enough to overcome the objections of the highest sticklers to those who actually worked at increasing wealth. This current venture was business as usual, as far as he was concerned.

Marlowe settled himself into a deep chair as Smithton braced a hip against the sideboard and swirled his brandy.

"You need to get some rest, Justin. You're still fatigued from our trip."

"It's this heat, Peter." Smithton grimaced as he took out his handkerchief and wiped his face. The humid air clogged his throat and made him long for the raw dryness of a winter's day. "I find most nights I toss and turn trying to find some relief."

Marlowe coughed into his hand. "You have to admit there are some compensations to our travels down the coast. Remember the ladies in Savannah?"

"Ah yes, Mrs. Fitzpatrick. She had the most amazing...indigo plantation. I was pleased to be able to meet in person one of Delerue Shipping's best customers." A fondly reminiscent smile crossed the earl's handsome face as he recalled specific details of the widow's person. "But you're right, Peter, all that being feted can wear one out. Well, we will be concluding our business here in a few days, and then it's back home."

Marlowe winced at Smithton's casual reference to his upcoming nuptials as another "business" transaction, but he knew which way the wind blew and cleared his throat.

"While you were attending to affairs with your soon-to-be uncle by marriage, I finished my reconnaissance mission..."

"You mean you got the tabbies in town to discuss my intended," Smithton muttered into his glass.

Marlowe inclined his head slightly. "Just so. The reports on Miss Christine Sanders were enlightening. Seems your betrothed will make a good dancing partner since she's described as 'overly tall,' and to be more specific, is near six feet."

Smithton, who measured six feet four inches in his tasseled boots, only raised his black eyebrows. "So my bride is long and lean. What of it?"

"Did I say she was lean?"

"Damn." The level of brandy in his glass dropped considerably.

"Actually, I'm assured Miss Sanders is of a size to keep you warm on winter nights."

More brandy disappeared.

"Further inquiry revealed her hair is a color that could only be described as...brown."

Justin carefully set down his glass and walked to the long windows that opened onto the enclosed courtyard. "Is there more?" he ground out, staring sightlessly at the gardens.

"Spots."

"What?"

"She has a spotted complexion."

"Dear Lord," he murmured, passing his hand over his eyes. "Did anyone have anything positive to say about her?"

"Yes, actually. More than one person admitted Miss Sanders has amazingly beautiful eyes—large, brown, and thickly lashed. And they said she was quick-witted and friendly."

Smithton walked back to the table and the brandy decanter came into play again. He gazed morosely at the contents of his glass.

"Large, spotted, with big brown eyes. Do you realize, Peter, that you have just described a cow?"

Marlowe stopped smiling and looked at his friend with concern. "Justin, surely there must be another way. In London, you wouldn't glance twice at this girl, and here you are, halfway around the world in East Florida, preparing to be leg shackled to her. Can't you marry one of the other chits who've been eyeing you?"

Justin stopped toying with his brandy and looked closely at his friend. Peter was aware the Delerue shipping interests were in trouble, but no one in London knew how bad the situation was, and Justin didn't intend to share that information. There were ships due in that had not been heard from and the company was dangerously overextended. He trusted Peter, but rumors of collapse could cause key investors to back out and that was a chance he couldn't take.

"We've been over that ground. I need the marriage portion Miss Sanders will bring with her and I need it quickly. Before you protest about 'other girls,' what you don't know is that our fathers pledged us to one another when she was still a babe. Apparently, my father was close to Daniel Sanders in their youth and because I was the second son, they thought it was a good idea to tie the two families together. Knowing how my father felt about me, I imagine he wanted me to settle in Florida, far away from England. It isn't going to happen now, but following the example of my forefathers, I've decided if I can't pillage for the blunt, I'll marry for it."

"But, Justin, surely now that you've inherited the title from your brother that agreement is no longer binding!"

Justin shrugged. "It is all the same to me. I need a wife with money and this one's available, even if she turns out to be *un peu grosse* for my taste. Look at the bright side, Peter—I can stick her on my estates and between the two of us we can breed a race of giants!"

Marlowe smiled at that last sally and rose from his chair. "Come along then. Now that you've bolstered your courage, it's time to retire to those charmingly rustic guest quarters to prepare to meet with your betrothed. Besides, I have faith the gossips *had* to be exaggerating. In this provincial part of the world, it must be grand entertainment to have an English 'milord' carry off a local girl."

The men's laughter as they exited covered the sound of the small gasp from the library loft.

Christine's shaking fingers bit into the binding of her book. She glanced blindly around the small loft, her haven ever since she'd been old enough to climb the ladder. It looked out the tall windows and over the top of the wall to the harbor and let in the breezes that made life in Florida bearable.

Christine slammed down her book of sonnets with an unmaidenly word. How dare he? How could that arrogant sod think he was going to travel all the way to Florida and drag her home behind him like a cow on a rope? She couldn't imagine leaving Florida. The Sanders family had fled here with other Loyalists during the war for American independence and prospered in the tropical setting. The Sanders orange groves were famous for the quality of the fruit and more Minorcans were being hired to bring in the crops and attend the trees.

Florida was home. Christine had traveled up and down the coast with her father and inland on hunting trips, always returning to the ancient city. She loved the polyglot hustle and bustle of a town that knew many flags, but managed to welcome all and make them a part of St. Augustine life. Daniel Sanders had been a vibrant part of that community, filling the hole in his heart left by his young wife's death with a dedication to two things—the Sanders legacy and his daughter, Christine.

What Christine wanted above all was not a beau but freedom—the freedom to sail her boat, make her own decisions, and manage her inheritance as her father had taught her. Becoming Countess Smithton and being stuck on an estate in Devonshire was *not* part of her plans.

The boats out on the water blurred through her tears. The conversation with her guardian in this very room a month earlier had made her future quite clear.

"You stupid girl, you ought to be down on your knees blessing me for this marriage!" Cliburn Beachum yelled, and Christine saw the disgust in his small eyes as he looked at his only niece. She'd heard him say to his friends that she didn't deserve her good fortune. She was to make a successful marriage, and Beachum was finally in a position to get *his* share of the monies his late brother-in-law had accumulated. Beachum had struggled along on his own modest inheritance, and small town gossip brought to Chris's ears tales of her uncle's bad investments draining away as he gambled and drank with his cronies.

He never married and was an infrequent visitor to his sister's home, so it came as some surprise to everyone when, as her closest male relative, he'd been appointed guardian of his young niece following her father's death.

The guardianship was carefully drawn. Beachum could live in the house and access sufficient funds for the upkeep of the estate, Christine, and himself, but he couldn't touch the bulk of the monies. Christine herself couldn't inherit until she was twenty-one.

Or until she married.

"It's not as if Smithton's getting a prize! Really, I almost feel pity for him. Look at you! Twenty years old, tall as a barn and about as wide! But make no mistake about it, girl, this marriage is going to happen, even if I have to blindfold Smithton at the altar."

He waved the letter from the earl raising the issue of a childhood betrothal.

"I have been waiting for my ship to come in all my life, and it's here. A Delerue ship. I'm looking forward to a comfortable old age, and no fat, mewling chit is going to stand in my way!"

Christine stared at her uncle. "I cannot marry a man I don't know and this Lord Smithton is a total stranger! You can't make me marry him!"

Beachum laughed and reached for his glass of brandy. "Don't be tiresome, girl. You can marry him, and you *will* marry him. I can make your life here very uncomfortable. There's no place for you to run to, and no one who'll believe you can seriously turn down this most attractive offer!"

"I can go to Uncle Julius! He'd take me in."

Beachum snorted. "That man-milliner? Hasn't been by to visit lately, has he? I made sure he had to leave St. Augustine after your father's death or face inquiries into his 'social life.' His well-known proclivities are a hanging offense." Beachum grinned nastily. "It wouldn't take much effort to revive the rumors of your father's *close* friendship with a known pervert. Let's see how respectable your father's good name would be after *that*!"

Christine sat still, her fists clenched. "Julius is one of the finest people I know. He was my father's friend, and he is my friend too. He would never allow me to come to harm."

Her uncle's thin lip curled into a sneer. "Oh, I know, Davies was a regular *nursemaid* when you were a child—but those days are past and *I* call the tune now. You'll do as I say and marry Smithton because if you don't, I'll convince the administrators at the lunatic asylum to make room for one more inmate—a young lady whose unruly ways and disordered mind make her unmanageable and in need of correction."

Christine raised her chin. "You won't get hold of my money if I'm locked away!"

He shook his head with mock sadness. "You're right, girl. I'll be heartbroken not to have a portion of the marriage settlement, but in the meantime I'll be comforted in knowing I'm enjoying the freedom of your father's house while cockroaches scamper across your dinner."

Beachum stood, still behind Daniel's desk, looking out of place in the neat library. His neckcloth showed remains of his breakfast and there was already an odor of drink about him. He looked down at his niece with narrowed gray eyes.

"This conversation is ended. In a few days your betrothed will arrive, you'll marry him, and your whining will become his concern. Or don't you remember what happened the last time you crossed me, girl?" He smiled coldly. "I see you do remember. Didn't get much help from the magistrate, did you, when you went running to him with your lies?"

Christine lowered her lashes, veiling her expression, even though she knew her pale face gave her thoughts away. She'd snuck out one afternoon to go to the magistrate and complain that her uncle had dismissed all her servants and she suspected him of mishandling her inheritance. Instead of being heard, her guardian had been summoned. Christine remembered all too well the feeling of impotent rage as she'd been forced into Beachum's carriage and dragged home.

And the whipping that followed her return to a house filled with strangers who ignored her cries for help.

"It's good that you remember, girl. You do anything to cause Smithton to break the betrothal and your last session in this room will seem like a Sunday picnic compared to what you'll get this time."

Christine sighed as Beachum's words echoed in her memory. Now her betrothed was here and it was worse than she'd feared. She climbed down from the loft and poked her head out of the library, praying she'd avoid the earl and his friend until evening. She had to find a way to get out of this marriage, even though she feared escape would be impossible. Her uncle had sold off her sloop after the whipping, and Christine suspected he'd be watching her closely until the wedding tomorrow. None of the servants were about as she ran up to her bedroom to think. Except for Cook, the servants were unfriendly faces, all newly hired since Cliburn Beachum had arrived and turned the old servants off. She couldn't count on any of them to help her leave.

She shut her bedroom door and leaned against the oak for a moment. The room was much the same as it had been in her girlhood. There were faded roses on the coverlet and shark's teeth on her chest of drawers. Her room was a hodgepodge of Spanish coins, fishing gear, a broken fan, and a plate of boiled sweets. She paced the dusty boards in front of her bed, avoiding looking into the pier glass. She hated the social functions she'd been forced to attend after her mourning was finished. While other girls had learned how to flirt and make conversation, she'd sat alone, "like a great pudding" as she'd overheard one matron describe her.

Worse was the pity and disgust in the eyes of the few young men who'd been forced to come and talk with her or ask her to dance. Being heiress to the Sanders fortune was enough to make her a good prospect in their mothers' eyes. She could have had three eyes and no teeth and she'd still be attractive enough, as long as her money came with her.

Christine picked up the plate of sweets and sat at her window, popping them into her mouth without tasting them. The air was quiet except for the drone of the wasps at the orange trees. This was the time of day when business and life slowed down as the brutal heat forced Floridians inside their thick-walled homes for relief.

If she could get to Julius, he'd help her hide for a while, maybe even for the remaining year until she could inherit her estate. She couldn't get to Julius without a boat and she only had a small bit of pin money—not enough to pay for passage to the cove where she knew he hid from St. Augustine society. Her only hope was convincing this Earl Smithton that she was unsuitable to be his countess. She wasn't optimistic. He wouldn't have traveled halfway across the world if he wasn't serious.

She pushed herself away from the window and walked to her small writing desk. Early in her life her father had said, "Life is full of choices, Chris. Some are good and some are bad. You have to learn how to make the right choice for you, and how to live with the consequences of your actions." He'd shown her how to make lists of her choices and weigh them in her mind to make the most informed decision. She looked down now at the sheet of foolscap in front of her and began jotting notes.

If I marry Justin Delerue, he'll have control of my inheritance. I already know he plans to stick me away in the country, so I can assume he doesn't want a business partner, only the capital. However, I'd be away from my uncle.

If I don't marry Delerue, my uncle will, at the very least, beat me and probably put me away.

She tapped her quill against her lip and looked at her notes while the insects outside her window buzzed softly in the sunlight.

What if I married Delerue, but didn't go to England?

Once she was married, her uncle would stop guarding her movements. And her new husband must be traveling with money for his expenses. If she could get away before her wedding night and hide, he'd have no choice but to seek an annulment. Eventually he'd have to go back to England to deal with his business concerns and would want a wife who could give him heirs.

The June heat was ignored as Christine began scribbling notes on what she'd need to make her escape. She already knew where she'd go.

Chapter 2

As night slipped over St. Augustine the evening breezes came in from the sea, bringing a welcome coolness along with insects that hovered about the candle flames. Justin and Peter were in the salon awaiting the arrival of Beachum and Miss Sanders, and Justin felt ready to face his intended. He'd dressed with special care, spending more time than usual to create something spectacular with his cravat. Justin's valet, Rogers, liked to fuss and complain about "milord not letting me do my job," but they both knew who was the master when it came to creating a work of art from starched cloth. Rogers had done a fine job this evening with the rest of Justin's wardrobe, easing the earl into a bottle green coat more suited to the English climate than Florida's wilting weather.

Justin hoped he wouldn't pass out while proposing. On the other hand, he mused, it might be a showy way of demonstrating to Miss Sanders the depth of his commitment to this marriage.

"My lord!" Beachum said, stepping into the salon with a forced air of joviality. "Allow me to introduce to you your bride, my niece, Miss Christine Sanders!" He turned back toward the doorway with a flourish and then, frowning, grabbed the hand of the still figure who hovered and practically yanked her into the room. Justin caught Marlowe's wince over the improper introductions and gave the young woman his most winning smile. She was dressed in a flounced pink muslin gown with a white lace overskirt, the furbelowed garment gathered under her full breasts by a silver ribbon. Her brown hair had been tortured into ringlets and silver ribbon threaded through it. There were indeed spots on her face. Unfortunately, a liberal application of rice powder only drew attention to this flaw. He wasn't unhappy with her height. It would be pleasant not to have to keep lowering his head and straining his neck to talk to her.

She briefly raised her eyes to his, and he caught his breath in pleased surprise. Miss Christine Sanders did indeed have extraordinary eyes, large and thickly lashed, and "brown" didn't do them justice. They were the rich color of the finest Spanish sherry, with gold glints in their depths. *Really,* he thought, *take some of that poundage off and the chit would be passable.* Not to the standards of the mistresses he'd kept in London, but good enough for his country estates. He took her hand and bent over it.

"My dear, it is a pleasure to meet you at last," he said smoothly. "Allow me to present Peter Marlowe, a close friend who's traveled here to stand up with me at our wedding."

Peter made his bow to Christine and smiled at her kindly. "This all must seem strange to you, Miss Sanders, but let me assure you that you're marrying a fine man. I hope you'll find your new life in England much to your liking."

Christine kept her eyes lowered and murmured an appropriate pleasantry to Marlowe. At least there was nothing remarkable about her manners, Justin thought with relief. Marrying an American was bad enough, but marrying a rustic American would have been too much, no matter how badly he needed her inheritance.

"Well!" said Beachum, rubbing his hands together, "Why don't we give these two a few moments, Marlowe, for Smithton to say what he came to say? Shouldn't take long, and then we can eat." Marlowe looked stunned at Beachum's lack of sensibility, but at a glance from Justin, followed the older man out. The silence left in their wake was numbing.

Justin cleared his throat. "Miss Sanders—may I call you Christine? Please, won't you sit down?" Christine nodded and sat on a brocade covered sofa, hands clasped in her lap, her eyes downcast. Justin perched alongside her at a safe distance. He made a motion to take her hand, but she only clasped hers tighter together. He took a deep breath and continued. "I know this is awkward for both of us, but as you are aware, it was our parents' wish we wed." She nodded again. "This marriage then, it is to your liking?"

She raised her eyes and Justin was again struck by their unusual color, but a moment later it was hidden behind the girl's lashes.

"I'm sure all will work out for the best," she murmured in a low voice.

"Well. Excellent." He winced. He sounded like that ass, Beachum.

"Christine, please look at me."

She raised her head and looked him full in the eye. For a moment he thought he saw a spark of animation—and something more—but it was gone and she appeared as before, a shy and placid girl. He deliberately softened his voice and smiled to put her at ease.

"We'll have plenty of time to get to know each other better. After a while, you'll see, it *will* work out for the best." She continued to stare at him, opened her mouth to say something, then stopped. She looked down at her lap again.

"As you say, milord."

Justin sighed and, as she stood, he rose and offered his arm and escort into supper. They took their seats in the compact and elegant dining room of the Sanders home. The high ceilings kept the worst of the heat away from the diners, and the fumes of scented oils drew the insects away from the tables.

Beachum was seated at the head of the table and Christine at its foot, and the intimate size of the dining room gave Justin a chance to study his betrothed. There was nothing lacking in her table manners, and he relaxed a fraction more. He still intended to establish her in the country, but she wouldn't embarrass him with her lack of social skills if friends came to call. He paused as he raised his wineglass to his lips. People *would* meet his wife, that was inevitable. He might have to spend more time in the country than he anticipated, making sure she fit in as mistress of Rosemoor. That could come after the financial crisis in London was resolved.

"Well," Beachum rubbed his hands heartily as the turtle soup was served. "Let us enjoy our supper and discuss tomorrow's ceremony."

"Oh, but uncle..." Christine protested. "Must it be so soon?"

"You'll be married immediately," he barked. "The vicar is prepared to receive both of you in the morning, and I know his lordship is anxious to have this business transacted quickly!"

Justin turned a charming smile to his fiancée, attempting to overcome her uncle's tactless manner. "Please indulge me on this, my dear. I'm needed in England as quickly as possible and we'll have a long honeymoon voyage to get to know each other."

She looked down at her plate.

"As you wish, sir."

For the rest of the evening, Christine deflected his attempts at conversation with monosyllabic answers. When her fiancé asked if she played the pianoforte or any other instrument, Beachum answered for her, as he sloshed more wine into his glass.

"Christine play an instrument? That's much too maidenly a skill for *her*. From what I hear, she spent her time sailing, fencing, and hunting with the low people her father kept about here!"

It was hard for Justin to imagine this overpadded young lady doing anything so physical, but he noticed the girl's fingers whiten around the handle of her fork at the talk of her father.

He leveled a cold stare at Beachum. "I'm sure my bride will be everything pleasing to me."

Beachum took a deep swallow of his burgundy and wiped his hand across his mouth.

"Well, to be sure, milord, the girl's not lacking in all womanly graces or the skills needed to run a household. After all, she served as her late father's hostess." He belched and paused to collect his thoughts.

Christine glanced at her fiancé. Smithton frowned as he turned the stem of his wineglass, listening to Beachum ramble about her shortcomings. She couldn't blame the Englishman for looking dismayed. Smithton was tall and good-looking, smooth mannered, and she could recognize the hand of London's finest tailors in his wardrobe. He must be a popular man in the London salons. She groaned to herself, imagining how society would snigger at the sight they'd make—the handsome, accomplished earl and his lumpish colonial bride. No one would ever think he'd married her for anything but money. No wonder he was ready to stick her in the country. With the other cows.

She sighed. If he'd been ugly, or messy, or maladroit she might have given the marriage a chance. Even stuck away in St. Augustine, she knew this was a mismatch of the worst kind. Florida merchants' daughters didn't marry peers of the British realm. Not if they expected anything good to come of it. Escape and an annulment was, indeed, her only option. In fact, the more she thought about it, the more she believed she was doing Smithton a favor by sparing him from having to stay married to her. She attacked her supper with renewed vigor, for she'd need all her strength in the coming days.

After supper Smithton asked her if she'd like to take a walk in the garden, or indulge in some other entertainment, but Christine pleaded a headache and the need to rest for her wedding day, bitterly noting the flash of relief that whisked across Smithton's face before he brought his expression under control.

Christine pulled back the curtain at her bedroom window and looked down as the two Englishmen left the guest house with a torch-bearing servant. She knew they were headed for the docks, and entertainment suited to a man's last night of bachelorhood. It would have been an opportunity for her to make her own escape, but as she'd expected, her uncle had other servants posted at the gate to make sure she didn't sneak out—and that Smithton returned and got to bed without injury.

* * *

Christine's wedding day dawned bright and clear, with birdsong and light breezes mocking her mood. Not wanting to waste money on a lady's maid, Beachum sent one of the kitchen women to help her dress, and the smell of sweat and bacon grease rolling off Grace Rollins flayed Christine's already raw nerves. Grace chattered as she pulled and yanked at Christine's corset. "That fella' o' yours shore is a good-lookin' un. Reminds me o' my second man, Jim, the one the militia shot for cattle stealin'. He was a big un too, and knew how to shake the sheets."

She chuckled at her own wit and gave the cords a final yank, then helped ease the gown over Christine's head. The dark blue morning dress of sprigged muslin had been attractive once, but that was some months and inches in the past. A pink wrap across her bosom strained at the seams and left Christine trussed like a sacrificial goose, red-faced and only able to take light breaths. The woman finally finished fastening the dress, briefly fanned herself, then pulled Christine's hair up, topping it off with a straw bonnet veiled to keep insects away. After an insincere "best wishes, Miss," she shuffled back to the kitchen.

Christine winced at her reflection in the mirror she normally avoided. How she looked in her wedding finery wasn't of concern, she told herself firmly. She gathered the flowers sent earlier by Smithton and paused in the doorway, looking back. This was the room where she'd spent her childhood and created special memories. She sighed, careful of the stressed fabric, and turned away, heading slowly down the hall. Tomorrow her husband-to-be planned to set sail for England. Tonight was her only opportunity to escape, and that was what she needed to think of. She patted the waist of her dress. The bottle of sleeping drops she'd stolen from Cook was still there, hidden in the little pocket she'd sewed in her underskirt.

Christine grimaced as she saw her uncle waiting to escort her to the church. From the looks and smell of him, he'd started celebrating the nuptials early and she desperately wished Uncle Julius could be here instead to walk her down the aisle. He'd understand what she was feeling and help her escape! As a child, she'd always been able to run to Uncle Julius with her problems. He'd picked the prettiest dresses, helped her with her hair, entertained her with stories of his travels, and taught her to sail. When she was thirteen and there was no one else she could ask, he'd blushed dark red and stammeringly explained why her body was changing.

Julius had been her father's closest friend and as she'd grown older, she couldn't help but hear the stories whispered about him and young sailors. There'd been occasional speculation too, about the widower Sanders and Julius Davies.

"*Honi soit qui mal y pense.*" Daniel used to grin and brush it off when the talk would reach him. He maintained discreet liaisons with certain widows in the town over the years and knew they gossiped about him, so the rumors about Davies and Sanders had never been taken seriously by those who knew them best.

At the Anglican chapel Justin waited, his brows raised when he saw his bride was alone save for her odious uncle.

"You bring no attendants, Christine?"

Her face clouded. "There was no one...here...whom I wished to have with me today."

He shrugged and turned to the vicar who was clearing his throat and preparing to join them in matrimony. Justin's mind was already moving past the ceremony to business concerns. If only the *Phoenix* and the *Griffin* had made it back from the Indies! He had the better part of his capital tied up in those ships and their loss made him cash poor and desperate. So desperate that today he was preparing to shackle himself to a girl who was not only unattractive, but possibly not very bright. He sighed. He *had* to have the money she'd bring to refit the ships he had in dock and hire the crew to take them out. No sacrifice was too great to save Delerue Shipping.

"Earl?"

Smithton was prompted from his reverie by the vicar to say his vows and bind himself to Christine Sanders. She never looked up, and kept her icy hand loose in his grasp as he tried to slip on a heavy gold band. The ring was too small and, after a moment's hesitation, he moved the wedding band to her smallest finger instead. As the final benediction was pronounced, he raised the veil from his countess's face and kissed her lightly on her closed lips.

They rode in silence to the Sanders house and in silence the small wedding party ate their luncheon. Peter Marlowe tried to make conversation when he realized Christine and Justin both had their thoughts far away, and Beachum was only interested in his wine.

"I was shaking my shoes out this morning and one of your native beetles entered into a tug of war with me over possession of my footgear," he joked, desperate to lighten the mood.

Christine smiled at his foolishness. "Our Florida wildlife can catch visitors unaware, sir. You may have gotten off lightly. The old men like to tell tales of mosquitoes carrying off oxen for later feasting."

Peter caught his breath. That smile transformed her round face, animating it and giving her chocolate eyes a sparkle. He thought with exasperation his friend Justin could be making more of an effort to get his bride comfortable with the idea of marriage. Instead, he excused himself early, saying he had to go to the docks to make arrangements for their journey, leaving Peter to entertain Christine through the long afternoon. Walks in the garden and a few hands of cards couldn't disguise the tension practically radiating from her body. So it was with a certain amount of relief that Peter watched her excuse herself to rest through the hottest part of the day.

Chapter 3

Justin washed in the tepid water left in his quarters, thinking toward the evening ahead. After having a peal rung over his head by Peter for neglecting his bride, he'd dismissed his valet and ordered supper served in his quarters. It would allow him to spend some time getting to know Christine and soothe her fears. His bride was clearly inexperienced, as was expected, but he didn't know if she was as ignorant of "marital duties" as most women of her class.

It might be best to get her wedding night over with as quickly as possible and he dearly hoped to keep her fussing to a minimum. Perhaps on the voyage home she'd learn how to respond to lovemaking. Based on her lack of spirit and wit so far, he wasn't optimistic. Justin shrugged mentally as he dressed in a linen shirt he left open at the neck for comfort in the heat. If his wife didn't like spending time in his bed, that's what mistresses were for. Few of his friends, from what he could see, turned to their own wives for comfort, preferring instead the mercenary relationships they established with opera dancers and widows. He couldn't imagine why his marriage should be any different from most marriages of the ton.

Shadows were filling the airy room as Beachum's servants set out his supper. He'd dismissed them for the night when there was a soft knock.

Justin opened the door and frowned to see his wife standing with her head lowered, clutching a small valise.

"I was going to come for you myself, Christine. It wasn't necessary for you to come to my quarters."

She looked up, startled. "Oh. Do you want me to leave?" she said brightly.

He sighed. "No, of course not," he said, swinging the door wide, and picking up her bag. "Come in, my dear."

Christine entered and glanced around the room. A lamp burned on a small table and the covers on the bed were already drawn down. She'd changed into a stomacher dress of sprigged muslin, a popular choice in the humid climate.

"Thank you for not insisting we dress for supper when it's just to be the two of us. As you can see," her husband said as he escorted her to the table and pulled out her chair, "I asked Cook to prepare a light meal so that we can become better acquainted. May I pour you some wine?"

"No...yes. Whatever pleases you, milord."

"What would please me is for you to call me Justin," he said, seating himself and pouring a glass of claret. "After all, now that we are married, there is no need for such formality." He raised his glass, smiling. "To u—"

"Wait!" Christine jumped up from her chair. "Uh, I forgot something in my room! Oh, mi—Justin," she said, wringing her hands, "Would you mind terribly going to my room and fetching my hairbrush off the bureau? It was my mother's and I'd be heartbroken if I didn't have it when we leave tomorrow." She batted her long lashes for extra effect.

"I'll ask one of the servants to bring it in the morning."

"Oh no, I'll need it," she cleared her throat. "For tonight."

He rose from his chair. "In that case," he said with a smile that hardly looked forced, "It would be my pleasure to run this small errand for you."

He shut the door carefully before stomping down the steps to the main house. Christine leaned her ear to the wood. When she heard the door to the main house close, she searched frantically through Smithton's belongings, laughing aloud when she found the pouch of notes and coins. Sifting through the mix of coinage from the United States and Britain, she took enough to make her escape and tucked the rest back into the bag. By this point she could hear footsteps leaving the house. She dumped the drug into her husband's drink, pulled her silver-backed hairbrush out of her pocket and sat.

She was gazing at the brush with a puzzled expression when Smithton returned.

"Now, isn't that strange," she mused, finger tapping her chin. "I could have sworn I left the hairbrush in my room and all this time it was in my reticule. Fancy that."

Justin's teeth snapped together as he held back whatever he'd planned to say. "I believe I'm ready for that wine now," he said, sitting and reaching for his glass.

"Oh, but what about your toast?" Christine asked with round-eyed innocence.

"To us!" he snapped. "And to many long years together!" Justin muttered something that sounded vaguely like "Lord help me" before draining his glass, the taste making him cough.

"Excuse me, my dear, this wine has gone bad; probably from the heat." He opened a second bottle of claret and poured again.

"Now, Christine, what would you like to talk about? Our trip? Your new home in England, perhaps?"

He served her from the dishes laid out for them: fresh snapper, chicken with an oyster stuffing, rice, and oranges from the Sanders groves. For dessert there was fruit and cheese and Cook's own lemon tarts.

"Will I be meeting your family in England, milo—Justin?"

"My brother and sister will be meeting us in London. I'm sure you'll like them." He smiled. She stared, fascinated at how a small thing like a genuine smile changed his face. He looked like an agreeable person when he smiled, the kind of fellow she'd wish to know better. If he weren't her husband, of course.

"Robert is getting ready to go off to Cambridge, and Suzanne has her head full of her first Season. They're thrilled I'm getting married and bringing a new bride home." He ran his finger slowly around the rim of his wineglass. "You mustn't worry about your adjustment to life in England, my dear. It will be a bit different, I know, but there are so many things to do at Rosemoor, you'll find yourself fitting right in."

"Rosemoor is your home?" Christine shifted uneasily in her seat. Watching that long finger running along the rim of his glass was making her feel uncomfortable. Damn, why weren't the drops working?

"Oh yes," he said softly, his grin widening. "Rosemoor is my country home in Devon, a lovely place set in rolling green pastures and surrounded by rosebushes. Their fragrance in the summer fills the hall. Christine," he said, reaching across the small table for her icy hand, "you don't have to be afraid of me. I know everything has been rushed at you. Once we're home, we'll hardly have to see each other at all."

He frowned suddenly and released her hand, rubbing his forehead. "Damn, that isn't what I meant to say…What I meant was…" When he looked up, his eyes were gleaming, his pupils shrunk so much she felt she was looking at a large and hungry jungle cat. "I'll do my best not to hurt you, and after tonight it'll be easier. You'll see." He grinned again. "I already like you better than I did before I knew you! You really do have beautiful eyes."

"My eyes?" she squeaked, apprehensive at his quick change in tone. "My eyes are ordinary brown!"

"No," he said, reaching across the small table to stroke his finger along her brow. "Your eyes are anything but ordinary. They're deep and have a color like the richest velvet. Christine...my wife," he stood and bumped against the table, swaying slightly. Justin shook his head, as if to clear it, then laughed. "My head feels as if it's floating away. Isn't that strange?"

Christine ran around the table, catching hold of him as he swayed again, knocking a wineglass to the floor, where it rolled to the door.

"Perhaps you should come and lie down," she said, leading him toward the bed.

"Lie down? A capital idea, my dear! I'm glad to see you taking the initiative in this. And aren't we fortunate you're such a strong, tall girl!"

She maneuvered her shoulder under his arm to help him.

"Just a few more steps and we'll be—LET GO OF ME!" Christine was flat on her back with her feet dangling over the side of the bed, Justin draped across her body. He began nuzzling her neck while his hands roamed along her rounded shape. "Le's wait on talking for a bit, shall we, m'dear?"

Christine panicked as she felt long fingers molding her curves. Drugged or not, her husband had every intention of consummating this marriage, ruining her chance at an annulment. Unfortunately, her struggles to free herself only inflamed him further. Her protests were muffled when he wedged himself between her legs and covered her mouth with his, slanting his head and swallowing her words. He held her wrists above her head with one hand while with the other he gently squeezed her breast, kneading through the thin fabric and flicking her tip with his thumb.

She wrenched her head to the side, gasping for breath. "No, Justin, wait, I'm not ready—"

"No?" He muttered, moving his hand from her breast down her luscious curves. He slipped it under her bunched skirts and slid it up her long thigh under her chemise. Justin stroked her lightly and she gasped at being touched so intimately. He grinned down at her, sweat glistening on his face, his hair falling forward and shadowing his eyes. "'S alright, *I'm* ready. I know what to do. Done it lots."

Christine thrashed her head and moaned softly. "Please don't do this."

For an answer, he lowered his head and began kissing her neck as he continued stroking her. "You don' want me to do this? Or this?"

His thumb was moving across her and when she futilely tried to scissor her legs away from him, he turned his hand over, brushing his knuckles across the entrance to her womb.

The tormenting hand moved away from the apex of her thighs and Christine heard the pop of released buttons as he freed himself. She renewed her struggles with fresh panic and bucked against him again, trying to dislodge the heavy body that kept her pinned to the bed. *It was all planned out,* she thought frantically, *he should have been asleep by now!*

All too awake and aroused, Justin released her hands and wrapped his arms around her, pinning her hands ineffectively to her sides as his hard muscled legs pushed her thighs further open.

"Shhh...hol' on now, Chris'ine, 'm almos' there."

She felt something probe between her legs and with one heavy thrust he was inside her. Christine cried out and arched up against him, which only pushed him in further. The earlier warmth she'd felt became a searing pain that grew as he forced his way into her body. She turned her face to the wall and his hot breath was in her ear along with muttered words she couldn't understand. He moved inside her, holding her close, smothering her, but she no longer struggled to push him off. Instead she lay there, dazed, as a voice in her head screamed, *Nonononono!*

Finally, with one last thrust and a drawn out groan, it was over.

Justin looked down at his young bride, the tears streaking her round face, and remorse stabbed at him through his fogged state. He knew something was wrong, and could not grasp what had happened, or why. But he knew he'd hurt her.

"Oh, Chris'ine...I'm sorry..." He heard the words coming as if from a distance and she appeared to be shrinking and falling away from him. He fell to the side, unconscious.

Chapter 4

Christine pushed and heaved at her husband's limp body and finally managed to dislodge him. She crawled out of bed and pulled herself to her feet. Her hand shook as she brushed hair back from her face and stared at the unconscious man sprawled across the rumpled covers. She briefly entertained the satisfying vision of running his razor across his neck and making herself the very wealthy *widowed* Countess Smithton. Instead she turned away with an oath and stumbled across the room, searching for her supplies. Wincing at the soreness between her thighs, she grabbed a cloth from the washstand, wet it, and viciously scrubbed away the bloody evidence of her new status.

So much for an annulment, she fumed, flinging the cloth to the floor. Some revised plans were in order, but the first business was to get away. She pulled out her valise and dressed herself in the man's breeches, shirt, and jacket she wore when fishing, tied her hair back and tucked it under her palmetto hat. The last thing she did was wrench the badly sized ring from her hand and leave it on the table. Shoving the money in her valise and wrapping the remains of dinner in a large cloth, she headed for the door.

Christine paused to look back at her husband. Asleep, he looked handsome and boyish and she felt a twinge of...*nothing,* she told herself. She leaned over, blew out the candles, and quietly shut the door behind her before easing her way down the stairs.

The twisting streets of St. Augustine were still in the night. A few sailors caroused at the taverns near the water and no one stopped the "fisher-boy" heading toward the docks with his gear. Christine allowed herself a small smile when she saw the *Lady C* docked in Manuel's slip. The Spanish fisherman had been taking good care of her sloop since Uncle Beachum sold it to him. She regretted having to take from Manuel, but knew she'd make the best time with her own boat. There was a vegetable stand near the docks run by Manuel's wife Rosa. Christine slipped a note apologizing for the theft and some money under the edge of the stand and directed them to her husband if the money wasn't sufficient.

Her gear quickly stowed, Christine untied the boat and with a local's skill navigated past the shoals and slipped away into a freshening breeze that carried her north to her destination. She didn't like sailing at night, but the nearly full moon cast enough light for her to navigate the coast to the St. Johns. There were few boats out in the morning, a few fishermen, some traders, no one whom she thought would recognize the *Lady C* as her boat. Manuel had painted over the name on the bow, but hadn't gotten around to making it his own.

The exhaustion of the night caught up with her shortly after midmorning and she began singing chanteys to stay alert. The sun beat down hot and her arms ached with the strain of holding the boat on course. She was thankful for the food and water as well as the wide hat keeping her from sunstroke. Fortunately the weather cooperated—she'd sailed this route in eight-foot seas and was in no shape now for that kind of effort.

By late afternoon the *Lady C* was utilizing the sea breeze to maneuver into the St. Johns River to a hidden cove near Cowford. It was an isolated, unpopulated area, shunned by the locals because of legends of a ghostly Spanish pirate who roamed beneath the moss laden oaks.

She stopped near a large boulder jutting from the side of the bank and sat quietly for a moment as the river lapped against her boat, listening to the mockingbirds and trying to pick out any human noises. Satisfied there was nothing and no one there, Christine threw the small anchor over the side and jumped into the water. She clawed over the roots on the bank and made her way to a cottage set so far back in the trees it was invisible from the river. Summoning a last burst of strength, she pounded on the heavy oak door.

There was a crash, and the girl stumbled back from the apparition that filled the doorway, a scarred ruffian, nearly a foot over six feet and bare to the waist. The pirate brandished a cutlass over his shaved head.

"Aaaargh!" he roared.

Christine's large brown eyes blinked once.

"Oh, Uncle Juuulius," she bawled, throwing herself into his arms.

"My God, man, you should be grateful! You've got the money and rid yourself of a wife you didn't want!"

Justin looked at Beachum in disgust, but the revulsion he was feeling for the other man was nothing compared to what he felt for himself. He'd awakened after his wedding night to a pounding head and a missing wife and remembered how he'd stared, puzzled, at the blood on the bedcovers. When the night's events came back to him, a search of the guest quarters showed that Christine and her small valise were gone, her wedding ring left behind.

The house and grounds were being combed for Lady Smithton when Manuel Delgado, clutching Christine's money, came to the house to report his missing boat and show Smithton the note from his runaway wife. Unfortunately, the fisherman had no idea where she might have gone or if she'd arrived safely. Peter Marlowe was dispatched to the docks to see if anyone had noticed the missing bride.

In the meantime, Justin wanted answers and literally dragged the protesting Beachum into the library to wring more information from him. Beachum crossed the room to the sideboard to put space between himself and the enraged earl, and Justin wasted no time in pleasantries.

"Christine didn't want this marriage, did she? What did you say to get her to agree to it?"

Beachum's hand shook as he poured himself a brandy and swallowed a large amount. "It should have thrilled the chit to be married at all, much less to become a countess! You saw her. Who'd want to marry *that* without inducement? Let's be frank, Smithton, the Sanders legacy is enough to make a man overlook the most distasteful of bri—"

The last was choked off as Smithton crossed the room and Beachum was slammed against the wall, rattling the liquor bottles as he dangled by his neckcloth. Smithton spoke slowly and distinctly, the white lines around his mouth emphasizing each word.

"You are discussing my *wife*, Beachum. If you ever make an uncomplimentary remark about Christine again, I will remove you from the ranks of the living."

He released his hold and Beachum fell to the floor, gasping for air. He pulled himself shakily to his feet, but wouldn't meet Smithton's eyes as he gulped for breath and continued in a hoarse voice.

"I told her any girl in her position would have to be *insane* not to want the marriage. If she didn't agree to it, she could bloody well spend the rest of her life in the lunatic asylum because I'd wash my hands of her! Really, Smithton," he sneered, putting a large chair between himself and the earl, "it's obvious she ran off on her wedding night because she developed such a dislike of you!"

Justin turned away, his fists clenched, only a massive force of will keeping him from throwing his uncle-by-marriage out the window.

"I want you out of this house by nightfall, Beachum. When Christine returns, I don't want you anywhere near her."

Justin slammed the library door behind him, but his steps slowed as he walked to the quarters where he'd spent his wedding night. It was quiet in the courtyard as he looked up at the guesthouse, the shade dappling over it in the late morning sun. He climbed the steps and looked around the empty room, then sat on the bed, now freshly made, and stared at the spot where the small table had been set for supper. He rubbed his forehead, still aching from last night.

Christine must have slipped him a drug, yet he remembered flashes of the evening. He especially remembered her body's soft warmth before he'd bungled things so badly. Self-loathing swept through him. Given a choice between marriage to a man whom she knew didn't want her or life in a lunatic asylum, the girl believed setting out on the open sea her best option. Beachum wasn't so far off the mark. Hadn't he also believed Miss Sanders would be thrilled at the prospect of marriage to him?

Justin brushed his fingers across the flowered coverlet. It was one thing to think of a bride in the abstract, and to concentrate on the benefits marriage would bring him. It was another to realize one was tying one's life to another, breathing human being. When he found Christine, he vowed he'd make it up to her, courting her with care and showing her that he wasn't the beast she thought him. Even if it was an arranged marriage, she deserved better from him than he'd initially been prepared to give.

Later that afternoon Justin was finishing his correspondence at Daniel Sanders's old desk. He was looking for a pen wipe in a side drawer when his hand closed round a smooth oval, and moving to the window he examined it in the light. It was a miniature of Christine. A good likeness, painted when she was on the verge of womanhood. Her slender face was dominated by doelike eyes, her lips quirking up as if she knew a secret and wouldn't tell, brown ringlets haloing her head. He gazed at it for a long while until distracted by a commotion from the front hall.

Christine! Justin thought as he slipped the miniature into his pocket and ran to the door, only to stop short. There stood Peter and alongside him, Henry Crawford, first mate of the *Phoenix*, his lost ship!

"Crawford! By God, man, I thought you were dead!"

Justin strode across the hall to grab the seaman's hand and pump it vigorously.

"Thank ye, sir, and I've come as quickly as I could because I've important news for ye." A grin lit the mate's homely face and he drew himself up to his full height to deliver his message. "Both the *Phoenix* and the *Griffin* docked in London and yer cargo is ashore. There was a merchantman bound for Savannah gettin' ready to sail day after we pulled in, and Captain Jackson dispatched me to bring ye the word right away that yer ships was safe and snug!"

The color drained from Justin's face and, for a moment, he wavered on his feet.

"The ships made it home? Dear Lord," he whispered, leaning against the wall as Peter ran to the library to fetch him a brandy. The cargo both ships carried was more than enough to rescue his ailing fortunes. Peter pushed the glass into Justin's nerveless fingers. Justin looked up and seemed to notice his friend for the first time.

"Poor Christine," he whispered. "A day later and she would have been spared having to marry me after all."

"What will you do now?" Peter asked sympathetically.

Justin took a swallow of the brandy before replying. "I have to return to England tomorrow as planned. It cannot wait, especially now that the ships are found. I can only pray my efforts to locate Christine will be successful and she'll join me soon."

"You believe she'll be found then?"

"I have to believe it, Peter. It is the only way I can live with myself."

Chapter 5

"We need to talk."

Christine paused, her hand poised over the planks she was scraping along the side of the *Tigress*, and smiled up at "Uncle" Julius Davies. In the fortnight since her arrival, he'd cosseted her, heard her story, and held her when she'd sobbed with relief at the proof she wasn't pregnant.

She pulled herself up the ladder to where he leaned over the rail and joined him on deck, reveling in the comfort of loose calico trousers and a once-blue shirt left behind by one of his sailors. She stretched in the late afternoon sunlight, feeling every ache in her muscles and the sweat plastering her shirt and camisole to her back. She'd worked harder this week than she'd done in all of the past year, but it felt good—and it kept her mind off the future.

Julius looked down at her fondly. "Let's call it a day, lass. I've brought a good ham back from town and we've fresh corn to grill with it."

Christine grinned and wiped her dirt-streaked face on her arm. "The ship is shaping up, Jules. She may be an old lady, but there's a bite in the *Tigress* yet."

Julius Davies preened as if her praise had been directed toward the vessel's owner. He rested his massive hands on his hips and looked about him with pride.

"Aye, girl, that worthless bastard who fathered me didn't leave me anything but this ship, and she's always been my one true love."

The *Tigress* was a 12-gun schooner, fast and sleek, made of good South Carolina live oak and built in New England. It wasn't bogged down with heavy cannon, carrying 12-pounders that relied on skill over size. There were dark rumors about how Owen Davies had ended up in possession of the sleek ship, but he'd been able to pass it on to his son freely.

In his younger days Julius had taken the *Tigress* all around the Florida peninsula, carrying various cargoes, some legitimate, some questionable. Though, as Daniel Sanders often said, "What was legal depended a great deal on whose flag was flying over us that day."

The only thing Julius wouldn't carry was slaves. His grandmother was a freedwoman who'd set up a chandler's shop with her husband in St. Augustine. They raised Julius when his Welsh father deserted their daughter shortly before she died giving birth. Owen Davies returned periodically to sell his stolen and smuggled goods in St. Augustine, and had taken Julius to sea with him when the boy was ten. Davies only wanted another crewman and an occasional snarl and cuff alongside the head was all the affection his son received. The Welshman met his end in a knife fight over a dockside whore, and at seventeen Julius owned the *Tigress.* His size and prowess with his fists quickly convinced the crew he was the master of the ship as well as its owner.

But the *Tigress*, like its master, was retired now, docked in one of the many deep inlets that fed into the St. Johns.

Christine put up her tools and scrambled over the side, relishing the cooling dip in the shaded waters before wading ashore. Julius's cabin too was cool and shaded, tucked back among the oaks, its wood weathered to a soft gray. It was a safe haven when the Indians and slaves rampaged during the Patriot's Rebellion less than ten years back. And while St. Augustine's population mix made it more tolerant than most communities along the Eastern coast, the threat of exposure and arrest for Julius was always real.

Chris helped her uncle in the detached kitchen behind the cabin, talking about the day's work, carefully not discussing the past or the future. She would catch Julius watching her and knew he was gauging her mood, but he said nothing about it while they ate.

Afterward the two sat in companionable silence cracking pecans, a mug of Cuban rum topping off a satisfying supper. Julius had his feet propped on the veranda rail as the red sun eased behind the moss laden oaks on the riverbank. A manatee frolicked in the water with her calf, disturbing a raccoon searching for his supper. Christine could feel the rum seep into her muscles, relaxing her after a grueling day holystoning the *Tigress.*

Julius broke the silence first.

"You're all anybody was talking about in town, Christine. There's a reward being offered for information about 'Christine Delerue, also known as Christine Sanders.'" The edges of his mouth quirked upward. "They call you 'The Runaway Countess.'"

"And Smithton?"

He cleared his throat. "Well, seems your husband sailed for England the day after you ran away. His people here are supposed to keep searching for you."

Christine said nothing for a few moments, watching the river flow north to the ocean. Finally, she sighed and took a drink.

"I don't like being married. I want my freedom."

"Being married is the way of the world for women," Julius said. "If Smithton hadn't run off so quickly, you maybe could have sweet-talked him into seeing things your way. Well, no use crying over what's done."

He shrugged philosophically as he poured another measure of rum. "So what should we do with you, Miss Chris? Maybe we could steal over to La Chua and make off with some cows and start our own herd, though I'm not sure I want to fend off gators for the sake of some beef."

"Do not mention cows to me." Chris wrinkled her nose in distaste. "I don't want to start over. I want Sanders Shipping! I hate giving up to that Englishman all my father built!"

"Christine," he said gently, "you didn't think this all the way through. No matter what you do, you no longer own Sanders Shipping. It all became your husband's property when you married." He watched her as the full import of his words struck home, and he continued like a doctor lancing a boil—a painful, but necessary task.

"If Smithton thinks you're dead, he gets to keep all your assets. If you send him word you want an annulment, which, incidentally, you have no grounds to demand, he could ignore you and he'd *still* have all your property and money. Even if he gave you the annulment or a divorce, he could tie things up in the courts long enough to ensure you get nothing but a bankrupt concern. And no judge I know of would favor your story over his anyway. The law's hard on women...and others who're different. If you don't return to Smithton, you're going to have to start over somewhere, doing something else, maybe even *as* someone else."

She leaned back in her chair and closed her eyes, absorbing the dusk sounds of the crickets and splashings in the river. Had all this been for nothing? A girl's foolish dream?

"Sometimes it's better to be someone else, Uncle Julius. Remember how we used to play pirates? If I *were* Anne Bonny like I used to pretend, I'd accost Smithton on the high seas and steal my money back."

It took a moment for her own words to penetrate her slightly fogged mind. Then she sat up straight and looked at Julius, her eyes wide. "Uncle Julius..."

He paused, his mug frozen halfway to his lips, eyes narrowed.

"I don't like that look. When you have that look, I usually end up feeling sorry about something."

"Why can't I get my money back from his ships..." Her face glowed with a new light as she imagined the possibilities.

He snorted and took another drink. "'Cause you're not Anne Bonny, and I'm not Calico Jack!"

"No, you're better than Calico Jack…you're Julius Davies, master of the *Tigress*!"

He smiled into his mug. "Need I remind you it's been many years since anyone shivered at the sound of my name? It takes more than a drunk old nance and a green girl to crew a ship!"

She waved away this objection. "We can do it, Julius. We can get my money back from that arrogant aristo. Maybe not all of it, but enough for both of us to be comfortable. And for me to be free."

He put his mug down on the rail, suddenly looking all too sober. "Child, have you considered what it means to run away from Smithton? Would it be so terrible for you to start a new life—aye, and a family—with him in England?"

The rum swirled in her mug as Christine stared into its dark depths. "I can't do it, Jules. I can't spend the rest of my life living with someone who despises me, or at best, sees me as a convenient means toward an end. Is it so much to ask for a happy marriage like my parents had?"

Julius gazed out over the water.

"What your mother and father had was very special, Christine. I don't believe many are that fortunate. Most of us have to struggle along on the fleeting moments of pleasure life gives us."

She abruptly stood and faced him, arms crossed before her. "What life gives us, Julius, or what we can grab for ourselves? No one gave my father Sanders Shipping—he built it into a company respected on both sides of the Atlantic. I learned how to manage the company from him, and it was *mine* until that Englishman snatched it away. Making do isn't enough for me, Julius. I want more. I want the life I was raised for!"

He came to his own feet and loomed over her, waving his hands for emphasis. "Do you know what you're asking? Even if you get your money back, you'll still be married! And look at yourself! What makes you think you have what it takes to carry this through?"

She straightened, her wide-legged stance making her look more like Daniel Sanders's heir than a runaway bride.

"I can't do it alone, but I know I can do it with you. We can put together a crew on the *Tigress* and go after Smithton's ships. I don't want everything back, that is unrealistic. What I need is enough to live on comfortably and pay a crew. And, with a few rich cargoes, we could do it."

"Piracy isn't make-believe, girl," Julius said harshly. "You could get killed or maimed. If you're caught, they'll hang you. Maybe your jailers will rape you often enough that you can be like your Anne Bonny and 'plead your belly' to cheat the noose till your bastard's born!"

Christine paled but said nothing, her arms crossed before her, staring at Julius and waiting for his answer. He lowered his eyes first, then with a slight shrug threw himself back into his chair and drained his mug.

"I won't make promises. I said you could stay here, and I meant it. Anytime you want to go back to St. Augustine and Smithton, I'll take you. But, if you want to follow through with this scheme, you'll do everything I say—and I do mean *everything*—and then we'll see where we stand."

Christine smiled and relaxed her tense shoulders. She walked over to Julius and leaned down to kiss his grizzled cheek.

"Thank you, Uncle. You'll see, I'll do you proud."

A month later, she was prepared to admit she'd died and gone to hell. Julius had her up before dawn each morning to scrape, scrub, and varnish the *Tigress* in the cool of the day. They'd break for dinner and an afternoon siesta when the heat was at its worst, then it was weapons practice. It had been a long time since she'd raised a foil with him, and it showed. There were days when he'd make her drill with knives, cutlasses, and pikes, yelling "it's not a bloody darning needle!" every time the point drooped.

"You need to be prepared to grab whatever is at hand and use it," he'd say mockingly, swishing the air with a cutlass she could barely raise. "You can't stop and bleat, 'Wait, please, while I get a lighter blade!' Only speed and skill will give you victory!"

Today, the drill was set on improving Christine's aim. Julius was leaning over a wooden wall he'd erected behind his house, casually swinging a glove at the end of a cord. In his other hand was a mug of ale.

"Again, *Cap'n*! If you can't hit that glove, how will you hit what you are aiming for when it's your enemy?"

Christine lowered her burning arm, panting. She swayed and batted at a cloud of gnats as sweat ran in rivulets off her face. With a small bit of encouragement, she'd faint where she stood.

"I can't do it," she gasped, looking at her feet, the ground, the glove, anywhere but at him. "I'm not strong enough."

The hated glove came to a stop in the still air.

"Right," said Julius pleasantly. "Let's step into the shade for some ale, shall we, and you can tell me about your plans for embroidering cushions in Devon."

For a moment, she stood as if carved from stone. Then she raised her arm, every muscle screaming in protest, but the blade never wavered.

"Swing the glove, Mr. Davies."

"Aye. This time, hit only the thumb. Fifteen times in a row."

At night they ate meals of fresh fish and vegetables from Julius's garden, and Chris was unable to do more afterward than collapse into her hammock in exhausted sleep.

Each day brought new challenges. On the days when the fierce rainstorms kept them inside the snug cabin, Julius had her study charts of the treacherous Florida Straits until she thought her eyes would cross. Her years of piloting small craft had only been the first step in preparing her to take the helm of the *Tigress.* There were his own maps as well, showing hidden coves and inlets along the St. Johns, the location of freshwater at Key Marquez where the merchant ships put in down the peninsula for supplies, and the locations where you were likely to encounter Indians.

She had to learn how to break down guns and put them together again, how to reload quickly enough to earn a barely satisfied grunt from her mentor, and how to hit what she aimed for, whether with pistol or musket. Soon she was adding her own contributions to the supper pot.

There were other lessons—

Julius stood in the soft sand at the river's edge, hands on his hips. "Always remember! A good big man will beat a good small man. Since you're smaller, you're going to have to be faster and more skilled than your opponent, because you can't put enough weight behind your blows. Now, come at me again."

"I think not," she said, wiping the back of her wrist across her face to clear sand and blood off of her mouth from their last round. Her shoulders drooped, and she looked at him defiantly. "I'm tired, I'm sore, and I'm not going to fight any more. It's time to call it a day."

Julius threw up his hands and began to turn away, not seeing her lightning kick to his belly. As he doubled over and hit the sand, he shifted his body, barely in time to avoid the foot trying to connect with the point of his chin.

"Enough!" He lay on his back, panting up at his grinning student. "You're sneaky, underhanded, and take advantage of your enemy's weakness. There may be hope for you yet, m'dear. *Now* you're beginning to think like a pirate!"

And there were lessons she never would have dreamed of—

"No!" he roared. "Widen your stride, *boy*! I don't care if all of Florida thinks you're my catamite, at least they'll think you've got a cock! You'll walk, sit, spit, and stand like a man! Now scratch your balls!"

"But they don't itch!"

"Lot you know about it! They always itch, so scratch!"

Nearly a year after her arrival at Cowford, they sat at the rough-hewn, well-scrubbed walnut table in the cabin. Christine was reviewing Julius's charts while he counted the money from a battered chest he'd dug up. A copy of the Delerue-Sanders shipping schedule poked out from under the chest, stolen from St. Augustine and passed up the coast by a well paid courier.

Julius looked out the window to the river where the *Tigress* rocked gently in the inlet, every inch scrubbed and polished till the brightwork gleamed. He leaned back with a contented sigh and rubbed the back of his neck.

"I wasn't sure you'd make it, but I think you're ready, *Cap'n*."

Christine frowned and chewed her bottom lip. She lounged back in a tall chair, her leg casually draped over the arm. "We've been over this time and again. You ought to be captaining this ship, not me."

He smiled ruefully.

"No, Chris, my time has come and gone. There are good men who will work with me, but we need someone new to rally them together, and I think you are that person. My being with you will give you the countenance you need and they will follow you. I can serve much better as mate of the *Tigress*."

She snorted. "Now you are the one who is dreaming, Mr. Davies. Who would follow a fat, gawky woman?"

Julius started, and stared at her. "You really don't know, do you? Come with me, girl, there's something I want to show you."

She trailed behind him to his room where a pier glass stood in the corner. Julius threw open the shutters at the long windows, filling the room with warm afternoon light. He pulled a reluctant Christine in front of him, facing the mirror.

"Look in the glass, girl, and tell me what you see."

She stared into the glass, and a stranger stared back. The stranger had hair cropped short for comfort in the heat, hair streaked gold from the sun. The body in the mirror was browned and pared to sleek muscles from holystoning and swordplay. Even the spots were faded. Only the eyes looked familiar, but appeared larger than ever under the short, tousled amber curls. She reached forward to touch the glass.

"I…didn't know."

Julius chuckled and squeezed her shoulders. "Well, now, wearing drawstring trousers will hide a multitude of sins. Haven't you realized how slack your clothes had gotten? No, my dear, when people see 'Captain Christopher Daniels,' they will see a tall, slender young man, perhaps a bit of a fop, with eyelashes a lass would kill for."

Christine looked again. The person in the mirror looked confident, strong. She smiled at her reflection. This was a woman who'd spent nearly a year transforming herself into someone who could make her own life, even if it was under a new and strange identity. She met her mentor's eyes in the mirror.

"You've thought about a disguise, then? I knew you wanted me to act like a boy, but I thought that was in case I had to run away."

"Aye, that was part of my thinking. If anything happened to me, you would be better off on your own as a boy hiding your true identity, at least until you could establish yourself. But now you are so much more than a helpless girl! I meant what I said about the men following you on the *Tigress,* and together we can make it happen. But first the mysterious Christopher Daniels must make a public appearance, and I know just the place to try out your disguise. It is time the captain recruited his crew."

The orangery at Rosemoor was in bloom. The fragrance wasn't as strong as the orange groves surrounding St. Augustine, but strong enough to put Justin in a blue funk as he dwelled again on what Might Have Been.

Nearly a year had passed without word. Everyone but him believed Christine drowned, and there was talk of suicide. It was a new and uncomfortable experience to be stared at when entering a room, to hear the pause in conversation, to know he was the topic of gossip. Before,

Lord Smithton had been one of the most eligible bachelors in London, no scandal adhered to him, the only tales told about him were those of the usual high spirits and activities of a young man on the town.

Now the supposed widower was shunned by many mothers of young women of marriageable age, even as those same girls avidly traded lurid conjecture over what had happened on Lady Smithton's wedding night.

But not all stayed away. Justin walked to the window and looked out at the orange trees, a cynical smirk twisting his lips. There were plenty of women who courted danger, encouraging him to enter their bedchamber and share whatever it was they imagined had traumatized his bride.

Despite that, he was still welcome in the drawing rooms of London society. Hostesses continued to send him invitations, no one shunned him at his club, and most importantly, Suzanne was still received at the homes of her respectable friends.

Indeed, there were plenty of people willing to overlook Justin's supposed penchant for driving young women to take their own lives, because it was common knowledge the presumed widower was very deep in the pocket. Justin glanced over his shoulder at the open ledgers on his desk. He no longer had to worry about lack of capital—between his wife's monies and the profit from his ships, Smithton and Delerue-Sanders were doing quite well. The *Manticore* would be leaving soon for Florida and he expected another tidy profit from the Sanders groves and other cargoes.

None of it mattered, though, except for the security it provided his brother and sister. Each night he sat in his study, drinking and staring at the miniature he'd taken from St. Augustine. If he couldn't find his runaway wife, he would spend the rest of his life knowing he had played a part in the death of a lonely young woman.

"If he becomes any more maudlin I...I don't know what," said Peter in exasperation to Lady Suzanne Delerue. Peter Marlowe had been taken on as a junior partner by Justin when the earl realized the combined companies of Delerue-Sanders and the extensive Sanders holdings needed more oversight than he alone could provide, and who better than his trusted friend to help manage the affairs of the companies? It had turned out to be a good move for both of them, Peter being adept at management, and the income providing him with a comfortable enough living that he could begin thinking about his own future. His own happiness was marred by the knowledge that his friend still suffered over the loss of his wife. He shook his head, thinking about their late night conversations about Florida and what had happened there.

"Christine Delerue was a pleasant young woman from what I saw of her, but she wasn't a candidate for sainthood! He's done everything but erect a shrine to her!"

"Justin's done that too," sighed Suzanne, her hand resting on Peter's arm as they strolled the gardens. "See that new area down the hill? It's known as 'La Florida,' in memory of the late Countess." She sighed again. "I didn't argue about postponing my season, but my goodness, Peter, I didn't even know the woman! And Justin only knew her for a few hours from what little I have been told. It wasn't exactly a love match. And though it's certainly showing Justin to be a man of great sensibility, I am worried about him."

Peter patted her gloved hand. "He'll make the season up to you, Suzanne. If you promise not to tell, I'll share a secret with you."

She looked up from under her chip straw bonnet, green eyes sparkling. "I love secrets, Peter, do tell!"

They paused in the shade of an immense walnut tree, and Peter smiled down at Suzanne. The ladies in America had all been charming in their own way, but there was nothing like an English girl to make a man glad he was home from his travels.

"Justin is planning to take the *Phoenix* back to St. Augustine. He's told me—in strictest confidence, mind—if you are a good girl, he will take you with us."

She squealed with delight, throwing her arms around her friend's neck. "Oh, Peter, thank you! A trip to Florida sounds wonderful!"

She stretched on tiptoes to kiss his cheek, but Peter had turned his head to speak. Instead of his cheek, her lips brushed his...and lingered. They both stood frozen as time stood still, then realigned itself in a new way. Peter stared down into her eyes, marveling at the color that rose up her neck to flood her fair complexion.

"Suzanne I'm..."

"Oh, Peter..."

They both began to speak at once, then both stopped. A moment later, Suzanne stepped back and Peter cleared his throat nervously. He ran his hand through his hair, disarranging the curls, and he found himself noticing things he'd never noticed before. She was more than his friend's sister, someone he saw on school holidays, and laughed with, and always found easy to talk to. She was his friend too. Then he frowned at the idea of her having a season in London where all the young bucks could ogle her. Perhaps it was as well they were going to Florida. This would give him time to think. There was a future ahead of him that had not been there before he'd achieved his new won financial security.

"We had better go back to the house," he said.

"Indeed." Suzanne opened her parasol, shading her further from his view and occupying both her hands. "You have given me much to think about today, Peter."

Chapter 6

It was a busy evening at the riverside tavern called Ganymede's Cup, a tavern with a reputation up and down the coast. It was that reputation that had earned the tavern its better known name, The Greek Boy, for the sign swinging over the door featured a young man in a skimpy chiton.

Simpkins, the innkeeper, stopped wiping a dirty rag over a dirtier mug, staring at the man stooping under the doorway.

"Why, Julius Davies, as I live and breathe! I'd heard you was hung!"

Julius smirked and rolled his eyes heavenward. "La, my dear, you don't know the half of it!"

His companion coughed delicately into his fist.

"Who's your friend?" Simpkins nodded in their direction.

Julius put his arm around the man's shoulder. "Allow me to present Captain Christopher Daniels. He's new to the area and I'm showing him the, uh, local sights."

Simpkins grunted, eyeing the tall, broad-shouldered youth. The young man had a low crowned beaver pulled down over gold curls, a smudge on his upper lip evidence of an attempt at growing a mustache. He wore an elaborately tied cravat, high collar points under a blue broadcloth coat, red striped satin vest, and foppish Cossack trousers tucked into boots. The man returned the innkeeper's stare calmly, hands relaxed, his right resting near a long dirk strapped to his thigh.

Simpkins grunted again. Davies's taste had always run to pretty sailors and this one seemed to be prettier than most, with those bedroom eyes. He shrugged and went back to wiping the mug. One of the things the staff of The Greek Boy did best was mind its own business.

Julius ordered drinks, "in clean cups, mind," and steered Chris to a table where they could sit with their backs to the wall and wait. A bored-looking serving girl brought their rum. She gave Chris an interested glance and an opportunity to pinch her shapely bottom. Chris smiled at her, then jumped slightly in surprise. The barmaid had a definite evening shadow underneath "her" face powder. Chris shrugged her shoulders and tipped her head toward her companion, who was nodding at some acquaintances. The "barmaid" pouted and flounced away for greener fields.

"'To have begun is half the job,'" Chris murmured, eyes also scanning the room.

"Indeed," agreed Julius. "I put out the word we'd be here tonight and I'm expecting company. Tonight'll tell us which way the wind blows on this venture."

Chris tilted back her chair to lean against the wall. It was a smoky, low room filled mostly with sailors. There were a few merchants and planters, judging from their dress, sitting in the darker corners. She took a small sip of her rum, dabbing delicately at her upper lip. If she could pass as Chris Daniels in this crowd, it boded well for the future.

Julius put his hand on her arm and nodded to the door. A man of middle height and middle age was approaching them, graying hair tied back in a queue. His eyes twinkled as he came closer.

"Julius, you old rogue, I might have known I'd find you with the fairest lad in the room!"

Davies chuckled and gestured at the newcomer with his mug. "Chris, allow me to present Thaddeus Brown, ship's doctor. And, unlike a lot of the others you'll find doing the bandaging 'board ship, Brown really *is* a doctor."

"Retired!" Brown said.

"Thad, this is Captain Christopher Daniels, master of the *Tigress*."

"Oho," Dr. Brown said, taking an offered chair and cocking his head to one side. "Been a long time since the *Tigress* put to sea."

Julius took a pull from his rum and glanced casually around the room. "Lower your voice, you're not on a quarterdeck. You know how it is, youth will be served, and Chris here wants to do a bit of voyaging. I thought you'd fancy a change 'bout now, Thad. Do you good to get out and about some more."

Brown snorted and waved to the server for ale. "I am all too aware of what you mean by 'a bit of voyaging.' We're both too old for this, Davies, and if I'd known what kind of rig you were running, I'd have sent my regrets. I am enjoying spending time with my grandchildren. I also enjoy not worrying about getting my arse shot off by some angry merchant objecting to how we redistribute his goods!"

Chris laid her hand lightly on Julius's arm to forestall any further arguing. "Julius tells me you served together when he was taking the *Tigress* up and down the coast," she said to the physician, her voice low and husky. "I understand you sometimes served as ship's cook also."

"I found if I was in charge of food storage and preparation, I had less disease than when I wasn't cooking. I wasn't the best cook in the Caribbean, just less likely to poison the crew."

Chris leaned forward and clasped her hands on the table. "Let me tell you why we're here, doctor. I'm going to take the *Tigress* out, for a limited run. There's a man who owes me money and I intend to get it back by…how did you put it? Oh yes, redistributing his goods." She flashed him an engaging grin. "I like that—sounds better than piracy, doesn't it? He's the only merchant I'm targeting and he doesn't suspect anything. I figure two or three hauls and we can all retire."

"I already am retired," Brown reminded her.

"Oh, and I'm sure it's a wonderful life," Julius snorted. "What do you do these days? Watch the oranges grow and listen to old ladies complain they can't move their bowels? Merciful Heavens, who'd want to leave all that?"

Chris leaned back and let the old friends wrangle back and forth a while before she banged her fist on the table, drawing their attention. She rubbed her sore hand and addressed the red-faced physician.

"Your reasons are valid, Dr. Brown, and I'll not try to talk you out of them. Here's the last thing I'm going to say, then you can walk away. I am going to get my money. I am going to get it from this merchant, and I'll do my best to see that every man who sails with me comes back in one piece and wealthier than when we set out. To do that I need a good doctor on board, and if Julius says you're the best, then you're the man I want."

Brown looked flattered, and resigned. "Much as it pains me to admit it, Cap'n Daniels, this old rogue does have a point. I imagine I knew something was in the wind else I'd not have come here tonight." He blew his breath out in a lusty sigh. "Give me the papers. I'll sign."

After signing aboard the *Tigress,* Thaddeus Brown took the captain's offered hand in a firm grasp, then turned it over with a puzzled frown, looking at the slender fingers and wrist. His sharp-eyed glance came back to Chris's face. She sat still, not breathing.

"Do you know, *Captain Christopher Daniels,*" he said softly, "I may not be the most brilliant physician to pass through the doors of Harvard College, but there are certain facts of anatomy I do know. I suspect you're not all you seem."

"That's our lookout," Chris said levelly, pulling her hand back. "Should it be of concern to you, Dr. Brown?"

"Well…I suppose it doesn't have to be a concern," Brown mused, rubbing his chin. "Do you intend to tell your crew? I know these sailors, and they won't take kindly to a captain who hoodwinks them."

"If it becomes necessary, I'll tell them. Julius and I believe it's better to have Christopher Daniels at the helm of the *Tigress.*" Chris smiled at the older man. "For now, I'm glad you've agreed to come aboard. I feel more confident with someone of your experience on hand."

The physician's cheeks flushed at her compliment and he cleared his throat. "I've spent much time alongside Mr. Davies here, and he's right—it has been too damn dull watching the oranges grow. I'm ready for a change!"

They talked for a while about stocking the ship with the supplies Brown needed, food and medicines, then the doctor excused himself when a morose-looking man with dark thinning hair approached the table. He nodded at Brown as the doctor left. The stranger seated himself with a glance at Julius, who announced, "Richard Cooper. Carpenter."

Chris waited for the man to speak, but he just sat, stonily looking at her.

"Right," she finally said. "I'm Captain Christopher Daniels of the *Tigress* and I take it you know Julius. If he vouches for you, that's sufficient for me. Do you bring any skills with you besides carpentry?"

"Fighting."

There was another uncomfortable silence while Chris waited.

"Right. You fight." She waited again, but when nothing further was added she said, "Here's the story then, Cooper. You sign on with the *Tigress* for a limited time. Could be a year, could be shorter. Sign the articles, take your pay, and meet us at the docks in a fortnight."

Cooper looked down at the articles, signed, took his dollar, shook Chris's now-gloved hand, and left.

"Cooper doesn't talk your ear off, does he?"

Julius's lips quirked. "He was in his cups once and I asked him why he was so quiet. He sat for a while, and I thought he wasn't going to answer, when he drawled, 'My pappy used to say, "Son, if you keep your mouth shut, they'll only wonder if you're stupid."' I do believe that was the most I'd ever heard him say at one sitting. Under that laconic exterior is a fine fighting man, Chris. I'm glad he's aboard."

Others drifted over through the evening, all known to Julius, and all but two willing to sign. One had gotten married in the past year, the other had started his own shop and learned to like life on shore. None of them had any particular objections to taking other people's money.

Julius had gone 'round back to relieve himself and Chris was idly balancing her dirk on her hand, trying to stand it on end. She'd almost succeeded when the table lurched, the knife fell, and she looked up with an annoyed frown into the face of a leering sailor. He planted both hands on the table and fell into Julius's chair, breathing ale and garlic fumes into her face. "'Ello, 'andsome. 'Ow 'bout buyin' a sailor a drink?"

Chris eyed him with distaste. "Go away. Now."

"Aw, c'mon." He winked at her woozily and leaned forward. "Fine young gennelman like yerself shouldn't be alone, an' it looks like your large frien's cut out on you."

To emphasize the joys of companionship, he put one grimy-nailed hand atop hers where it rested on the table. His other hand was under the table, beginning an unsteady foray up her thigh. Chris shifted her leg away and grabbed his neckcloth from under the table, pulling down, hard. The persistent Romeo's chin hit the tabletop with a satisfying thud and his eyes rolled back in his head.

"Oh, innkeeper," Chris drawled, fluttering her hand for emphasis, "There's some trash that needs to be removed."

Simpkins grumbled as he came around to retrieve the inert sailor, but pocketed the coin Chris held out as he dragged the man away. Julius passed Simpkins at the door.

"Trouble?"

"Nothing I couldn't handle," she said, adjusting the lace at her wrists. "After all, a good-looking bloke like Captain Christopher Daniels has to be prepared for that sort of thing."

The hour was growing late and she rubbed her hand over her eyes. Twice she'd gone 'round back and used the ingeniously carved gourd pinned inside her trousers. It allowed her to stand up like the other tavern patrons rather than hunt for bushes. The gourd made sitting a delicate operation, but it did provide a convincing appearance to the front of her pants—even if Julius had dryly accused her of "bragging" when he'd first seen it.

"Hang on, Chris, I'm expecting one mo—yes, there he is now."

There was a commotion at the entrance to the tavern. A man stood in the doorway, the dirtiest man Chris had ever seen, but that wasn't so remarkable. What was remarkable was the large gray goose with a jaunty red ribbon around its neck cradled under his arm.

Simpkins looked up.

"Hey! You can't bring that pig in here!"

"That's not a pig, you idjit," the man roared. "This here's a goose!"

"I was talking to the goose!"

The dirty man growled at the laughter rolling around the tavern. Cradling his bird close, he made his way to the back table where Chris sat. The crowd parted before him like the Red Sea parting before an odoriferous Moses. Chris had her scented handkerchief out and over her nose before he stopped at the table. There were distinct advantages to playing a fop.

"Captain Daniels," Julius coughed, "Meet 'Gunner Goose' Howe. And his companion, Sally."

Chris gasped at the man's eye-watering stench, but said, "Gunner. Uh, Sally. Have a seat."

Howe sat and placed Sally on the floor where she eyed the tavern patrons warily.

"I'm looking for a man who knows cannons," Chris said and filled Howe in with the plans for the *Tigress.* He scratched his beard meditatively, no doubt disturbing entire colonies of wildlife, Chris thought.

"Agreed," Howe said, "But where I go, my Sally goes."

"I have no objection to the goose as long as you take care of her," Chris said, giving him a hard-eyed look. "I have one condition that isn't in the articles, Mr. Howe. Before you set foot on my ship, you'll bathe yourself and your clothes, and you'll bathe at least once a month thereafter."

Howe started to howl about the dangers of bathing, but Chris cut him off. "That's all, Mr. Howe. Take it, or say good night. And, if you disobey these orders on board, you will find keelhauling is not a lost art!"

Howe muttered darkly about agues and chills, finally put his mark on the papers, and took his dollar. Collecting Sally, he stomped out of the tavern. Chris breathed a long sigh as she gave Julius a sidelong glance.

"How close are Gunner and his goose?"

"You know the story of Leda and the Swan?"

"Never mind." She sat back and closed her eyes. "Will I be able to keep up this masquerade in front of my crew, Julius?"

"I don't know. Will you?"

She chewed on that for a few moments. "I believe so. The captain is apart from the crew most of the time anyway. My cabin has its own head and no one'll expect me to use common facilities. You as First Mate gives me a buffer. I think we can manage it."

"It won't be easy, Chris. You knew that."

She pushed off the plank seat and stood, stretching cramped muscles and trying to ease the ache in her tightly bound breasts.

"Nothing worth having is ever easy, is it Jules? You and Father taught me that many years ago. Smithton thought he could do the easy thing by marrying the Sanders's heiress. We're about to teach him how wrong he was."

Chapter 7

The *Manticore* was three days from Florida landfall when it was hailed by the passing schooner. It had been a rough crossing, with storms whipping the vessel and tongue lashings for the sullen crew.

Captain Oswald Ryan peered through his glass at the approaching ship. He spent a moment admiring the three fashionably dressed young ladies along the schooner's rail, peeping from underneath their parasols and waving at the British merchantman.

"By Jove, there's a pretty sight to greet a sailor," Ryan said to himself before raising his horn to answer the hail. "The *Manticore* out of London, headed for St. Augustine. Who are you and where are you bound?"

"We're the *Tigress* under Captain Christopher Daniels, bound for Boston. Will you heave to and carry messages to East Florida?"

Ryan passed his glance over the *Tigress,* a trim ship flying Venezuelan colors and carrying passengers and light cargo from the way she rode. He agreed to bring a boat to the *Tigress*, and said he'd be pleased to take a glass with Captain Daniels. He headed down to his cabin, snarling at a sailor who didn't move out of the way fast enough, but his steps were dogged by his first mate.

"Begging your pardon, Cap'n," Jensen said, "don't you want to send one of the officers over to exchange pouches?"

"Quit being such an old woman, Jensen," Ryan scowled into the mirror, rearranging his thinning hair into curls. "We aren't involved in hostilities with Venezuela! Didn't you see those young senoritas? 'Pon my word, now there's a trio of lookers! My going over is the proper thing to do—show them how a real gentleman behaves, not like those jumped up Yankees!"

Jensen frowned again and said nothing. Ryan's temper was notorious and he treated officers and men with equal contempt. Jensen hoped for a long and productive career with Delerue-Sanders, especially with the new ships added on by the owner's marriage. He couldn't advance himself, though, if Ryan spoke out against him, so Jensen kept his thoughts on overly friendly passing ships to himself.

The schooner maneuvered within rowing distance of the

merchantman and soon a boat was made fast to the *Tigress*. A light tropical breeze ruffled the cloth at Ryan's throat, while overhead gulls called raucously to one another at the sight of the tall ships so close. Captain Daniels stood at ease in a green striped coat and yellow trousers, a casually tied ochre cravat rounding off his flashy appearance. Daniels greeted Ryan and his pair of crewmen with a warm smile and took the pouch, passing it to a hulking bald officer at his right shoulder.

"This really is very good of you Captain…Ryan, is it? Thank you for joining me. We don't get much company on these voyages, and it's always a pleasure to spend time with another captain."

Daniels motioned to a sailor who poured a brandy for each. Daniels sniffed appreciatively at the bouquet and held it up to the light, admiring the color, then set the glass back down with a small *clink* and smiled at his guest.

"And now, Captain Ryan, since you were nice enough to join me on the *Tigress*, I'm sending my men to the *Manticore* to have a look at your manifest."

Ryan choked, spraying fine French brandy on the deck.

"The manifest?" He stepped back and eyed the *Tigress's* sailors now enclosing him in a semicircle. "Why do you want to see our manifest?"

"Because it will make removing your cargo that much more efficient. I like efficient operations, don't you?"

"Don't be ridiculous!" Ryan blustered. "You can't sail up and take my cargo!"

"I'm afraid I must disagree," Daniels said, punctuating his sentence by languidly gesturing to the giant, who bellowed, "Show 'em what we've got, boys!"

The *Tigress's* crew moved back from where they'd blocked Ryan's view of the starboard guns, primed and trained on the *Manticore*, the gunports now flung wide. The three "ladies" produced wicked-looking cutlasses from under their skirts, proving, up close, they were hardly ladies at all. Shouts rose from the *Manticore* as the Venezuelan flag was run down and replaced by a black flag with a white tiger's head, its mouth opened in a snarl.

Wild-eyed, Ryan swung back to stare at Daniels. They both knew the *Manticore* was hopelessly outgunned and unprepared.

"Just so," Daniels murmured.

"You'll all hang for this!" Ryan swore, beginning to feel real fear.

Captain Daniels pulled a lace handkerchief from a finely tailored sleeve, sniffed delicately, and sighed. "Really, Captain, that is *so* predictable. Let's keep this simple, shall we? Have your officers round up your crew while we unload your cargo, and I won't blow your ship to kingdom come."

Ryan spluttered, but the prod of a cutlass in his side produced the necessary actions. He hailed his ship and told Jensen not to resist. Sweat poured down his back as he contemplated which would be worse—being disemboweled by pirates or having to face Lord Smithton with news of the robbery. And then he watched helplessly as the boats traveled back and forth, taking his cargo and career.

The *Tigress's* crew was in high spirits while Julius directed them in the unloading of silks, tea, brandy, dinnerware, and other goods from the *Manticore*, including a suitably heavy strongbox from the Captain's cabin. They left the personal effects of the crew and officers, but helped themselves to their fine weapons. There were a few minor skirmishes with the *Manticore's* officers, and the *Tigress's* crew put them down with a minimum of fuss.

Chris grinned wildly, the blood singing in her veins. After all her careful planning, the excitement of actually robbing Smithton's ship was as potent as fine wine. The deck of the *Tigress* hummed with activity while her men transferred the loot. She was beginning to think she could breathe normally again when a yell from the stern drew her attention, and she saw Captain Ryan struggling with Cooper over possession of a dirk. Chris sprinted across the deck as Cooper twisted the captain's wrist. The older man howled and dropped the knife and Ryan stopped struggling with Cooper when two of the *Tigress's* pirates grabbed his arms.

He strained against their hold and screamed at the young sailor from the *Manticore* who'd yelled out the warning, "You whoreson bastard! I'll flog your back off for this!"

"Are you injured?" Christine asked Cooper, who'd stooped to retrieve his knife.

"No," the carpenter said tersely and jerked his chin toward the sailor. "Thanks to Robin."

Her brows arched. "You two know each other?"

"Aye. St. Augustine. Gormless twit."

"Hello, Richard," the sailor said, eyeing Cooper nervously and shifting his weight from foot to foot. Chris cleared her throat. Loathe as she was to interrupt this touching reunion, she had a ship to sail and a cargo to dispose of.

"What's your name, sailor?"

"Robin, sir, just Robin," the slight youth replied, tugging a curly blond forelock.

"Well, Master Robin, I appreciate your warning Mr. Cooper." She rubbed her cheek thoughtfully. "It wouldn't be prudent for you to stay aboard the *Manticore* now. I can give you passage or take you on as crew. I'll be blunt with you, boy…why should I trust someone who turns on his captain to help a pirate?"

"I'm not a boy, sir," Robin said, affronted. "I've got twenty-two years and, beggin' your pardon, sir, but I'll be damned if I'd let that sorry bastard Ryan stab the back of someone...of a friend. Ryan's a mean'un, sir, and if you'll have me, I'm ready for a change for, sure as I'm standin' here, he'll have me hung or flogged to death."

Chris mentally agreed with his assessment. She folded her arms and frowned fiercely.

"Very well, Mr. Robin, we'll take you aboard—but know this, I run a tight ship and a loyal one. Try any tricks here and you'll find yourself left on a convenient sandbar. What are your duties on the *Manticore*?"

"The cook, sir."

Chris eyed him with new interest. "Really? So happens I could use a cook. Mr. Cooper!"

"Sir?"

"Mr. Robin is now your responsibility, seeing as how it was your hide he saved. Retrieve his belongings when you escort Captain Ryan back to his vessel." She turned to a man standing aft. "Doctor, take our cook below and check him out. If his standards aren't to your satisfaction, correct them."

Chris stood recklessly exposed at the rail as the two ships separated and the *Manticore* moved off for the remainder of its interrupted journey. She ordered extra rum for her crew, a move that got her a rousing cheer as the *Tigress* set a course south to unload its cargo.

"Mr. Davies, please join me in my cabin."

"Aye, Captain!"

Julius closed the hatch behind them while Chris lurched across the cabin to the head, where she gave up the remains of her breakfast. He carefully ignored her and retrieved the bottle of rum on her desk, pouring them each a dram. Chris came out white-faced, but composed. She rinsed her mouth and sat on the captain's oversized bunk, not speaking until she'd downed enough rum to halt her hands' trembling. She stopped Julius with her fingers over her glass when he went to pour her another.

"I thought I was going to embarrass myself and get sick in front of the crew. I have never been so scared in my life."

"You and me both, Captain. I can't believe we did it."

She stripped off her jacket and turned her back to unstrap the sweat-soaked bindings around her breasts, then rebuttoned her shirt and stretched luxuriously. "You can't imagine how good it feels to take that off and breathe again, Jules."

She flopped onto her bunk, staring at the deck above, hands beneath her head. Julius sat astride a chair and looked at her fondly. "You did well today, Chris. Your father would be proud."

She turned her head and looked at him askance, one eyebrow raised. "My father would be proud that I robbed and terrorized a ship?"

"No, girl." He chuckled. "He wouldn't have approved of that. But he would have been proud to see you in command, making decisions, and not showing a whit of fear. You did the right thing to take on that boy too. Ryan would have killed him."

"I know." She sighed. "I felt like I had no choice in that—after all, he did save Cooper when he could have kept his mouth shut. Hopefully, he won't find the *Tigress* uncomfortable."

"I've a feeling he'll fit in," Julius said dryly. "If not, you can drop him off as promised."

"Any thoughts on how much we may have gotten today?"

Julius rubbed the stubble on his chin. "We'll have to give it a thorough accounting, but I'd guess, with the strongbox over there, we may have enough to cut short our life of barratry. If Smithton keeps shipping cargoes as rich as this, it will only take a couple more good hauls and you can quit, Chris."

"I hope so, Jules. I want the money, but I don't want anyone hurt. We were fortunate today."

"It wasn't just fortune, Captain. You planned this foray, and while plans don't always work out once the bullets start flying, you used your brains rather than your guns to accomplish your goals. These waters are overrun with men who aren't bright and depend on brute force to gather money. You are using a better way. And with a ruse like this, you are less likely to attract the attention of the authorities. I imagine by the time Captain Ryan returns to London, he will have a story of bravado and fortitude prepared for his employers. Not a tale of how he was tricked out of his cargo. Speaking of which, I know some men in Havana who'll give us a good price for the goods and not ask questions."

"Give the order then to head for Cuba, Mr. Davies."

"Aye, Captain. And again, congratulations on a successful foray. You have proven your mettle to your crew."

And to yourself, he didn't need to add.

Being a pirate carried some of the same problems found in any legitimate business. Christine Delerue had a product—in this case, the cargoes of other ships—and she needed to sell it for a profit. That's why there were cities like Havana.

Havana was far enough from the government in Spain, yet close enough to Florida, to make it an attractive destination for seafarers in need of merchants who asked no embarrassing questions. It was only a few years since Havana was allowed by the Spanish to ship its sugar, rum, tobacco, and coffee directly to any part of the world, and the merchants in the Caribbean were hot to take full advantage of the new opportunities.

The *Tigress* crossed the Florida Straits in good time and docked in Bahía de la Habana for three days while Julius and Captain Daniels negotiated with the merchants.

"Bandits, the lot of them!" Julius grumbled, clearly ignoring the irony. "However, we're doing better than I expected, so I won't complain too much."

They made a good bargaining team, Chris thought. Captain Christopher Daniels would talk in his soft drawl, drawing on years at Daniel Sanders's knee while he parleyed goods into gold. Julius would sit alongside her, looking fierce. When it came to the sticking point, Julius would growl words like "thieves...unpleasant accidents...fires...warehouses damaged..." all the while fondling his dirk. Chris would shrug as if to say, "I can't control him," and prepare to go elsewhere. The merchants usually came 'round with another offer.

Chris was well satisfied this evening as they crossed the Plaza de Armas to their inn. "Maybe if you filed your teeth into points, all you'd have to do is open your mouth and smile and they'd pis—hello, what's this?"

A seaman had a young woman pinned against the Castillo Real wall and was gripping her shoulder while beating her with his fist and kicking at her. The girl had her arms wrapped around her head to protect it while sobbing for mercy in Spanish.

"Where are the guards?" Chris asked, already moving toward the couple.

"Ignoring this, as we should be!" Julius sighed, but he too hurried. Christine took advantage of darkness and surprise to grab the assailant by the back of his coat and yank hard, throwing him up against the wall. The Spaniard recovered quickly, though, and came up with his knife in hand. Chris jumped backward, grabbing for her own knife, as the man grinned and thrust with his dirk. The hours of training in the sun paid off. Chris crossed her arms low, creating an *X* that caught the man's arm as he thrust at her belly. Her left hand grabbed the wrist holding the knife and pulled, while her right knee came up hard into her opponent's belly. The *chink* of his knife hitting the wall was followed a moment later by the thud of Julius's hamfist against the side of the man's head.

"Nice of you to join us, Mr. Davies!" Chris panted as her opponent went down like a gaffed flounder.

"Dammit, gir—Captain, you've got moss for brains, plowing in like that!"

"Not *now,* Julius! Help me over here."

Christine knelt and rolled the fallen young woman over. She winced. The girl's face was a mass of bloody cuts and smeared paint, and her eyes were already swelling shut. She was still babbling in Spanish and Christine responded in the same language.

"Shhh...softly now, he cannot hurt you." She motioned to Julius who hooked his arm under the girl's slim shoulders and hoisted her to her feet. She wavered for a moment, then managed to stand, cradling her side. She was crying now and clinging to Julius's arm.

"I don't know why he kept hitting me, I said I'd do whatever he wanted...I needed money for the rent..."

Julius mouthed "whore" over the girl's head. Christine rolled her eyes.

"Thank you, Mr. Davies, I'm not an idiot." She pulled out her handkerchief and passed it to the prostitute, who muttered her thanks and wiped her face. "Can you manage to get home by yourself?"

"*Sí.* Thank you for your assistance." She looked down at her assailant, who was beginning to stir, and shuddered. "That one, he would've killed me. I will remember you in my prayers, Captain."

Christine dug a coin out of her pouch and flipped it to the girl, who caught it with the ease of practice.

"Take that and go home now."

The battered prostitute mumbled thanks again and shuffled away, showering blessings on Chris, her crew, her big friend, and every one of her relations.

"*Maricones*!" The man was conscious and sneering, cradling his jaw as he looked up at them with small eyes. He started to say something else, but stopped when Julius lightly and methodically tapped his fingers against his knife sheath.

Christine arched one brow at the man on the ground. "Dear me. I did not think we had been introduced, Senor…?"

The sailor leaned against the grimy wall and pushed to his feet. "I know who you are! Everyone knows about the Americans from *Tigress*. You better get out of Havana, or I, Ramon Ramirez, will make you pay! When I tell my crew of this insult, your life won't be worth two centavos in this town, pig! You, and the others like you!"

Christine flashed her own dirk and held it under the Spaniard's chin, raising the point until it indented his skin. He froze. "I've heard of you too, Captain. You, Ramirez, are a drunken idiot. And a bully. I don't like men who beat women and you'd better hope I never see you or any of your scurvy crew sniffing around *my* ship."

She added a bit more pressure with her knife for emphasis and the sweat of fear mingled with the fumes of alcohol and cheap cologne rolling off the man. She abruptly stepped back.

"Come, Mr. Davies. We have seen enough of Havana for this evening." She deliberately turned her back on Ramirez, a calculated insult, before striding back to the docks. Julius, a survivor of more fights than Christine had teeth in her head, kept an eye on their foe until they were well out of pistol range.

After boarding the *Tigress*, Christine had a few words with the men on watch to warn them of possible trouble from Ramirez's crew. She joined Julius forward of the galley where it was his habit to smoke a bowl before retiring for the evening.

"We need to head back out, Jules. Ramirez might decide our presence is more than he can bear, and I don't want anything distracting us now."

Davies looked at his protégé for a long moment. "Have you thought about what you'll do when this is over?"

She stared at the town for a few heartbeats, then sighed. "No, I haven't. Getting to this point has taken all my energy. I don't know where I'll be when this is over."

"What if there's no divorce, Chris?" he asked softly.

She stared at her hands, toughened and scarred by her life at sea. "I don't know, Jules. It's getting hard to imagine having the kind of life I used to dream about—a *real* husband, a home, someone by my side building a life with me. I would never be able to explain any of this. Even if I got a divorce from Smithton, most men would consider me damaged goods." She smiled ruefully. "When all was said and done, Anne Bonny died alone, didn't she?"

"Merciful Heavens, we aren't to that point yet, Captain!"

"No, you're right, Jules." She smiled again, a genuine smile. "Seeing that poor girl tonight put me in a dark mood. At least Captain Daniels managed to make someone's life a little easier, if only for a brief while."

With that, she wished her friend a good evening and headed to her cabin and her solitary bunk.

Chapter 8

"Pirates? The *Manticore* was taken by pirates?"

"Only the cargo," Peter Marlowe said, laying the papers in front of his friend and employer. "This was just sent down from London. The ship itself is unharmed, and it appears the crew came through unscathed as well."

"That, at least, is a blessing," Justin said, coming out from behind his desk. He picked up the papers and scanned through them, then stopped and looked at Peter.

"Where's Captain Ryan?"

"Already signed on with another ship, and has tendered his resignation. It's in the back of that bundle," Peter said, motioning toward the sheaf Justin held. "I haven't spoken to Jensen, but the word in London is Ryan was so upset over the idea of facing you, he decided to cut his losses and run to China. Some of the crew deserted to join—" He looked down at the letter he held. "—this pirate, Christopher Daniels."

"Good riddance." Justin grimaced, throwing the ill tidings on his desk and running his fingers through his hair. "I was warned piracy in the Indies has worsened since the war ended. Spain's policies make it all the more attractive for pirates and so-called privateers to ravage merchant shipping. This Daniels is just one jackal among many."

Peter picked up the discarded papers and leafed through them. Now that he was a partner at Delerue-Sanders, he had a better grasp of the needs that had driven Justin into his ill-fated marriage. This entire affair, the marriage, Christine Sanders running away, rebuilding the shipping line—all of it had taken its toll and Justin had changed. He was a grimmer man than he'd been a year ago. One with new lines on his face, and a new determination not to fail.

"It wasn't as much of a concern to Delerue Shipping alone, but Delerue-Sanders has substantially increased your traffic between the West Indies and England," Peter said. "Shipping in those waters remains a good move for you, unless your insurance costs and losses drive the company back into debt."

"I could send the ships in convoy. That's not as efficient, and in the long run the delays will be costlier. The Americans have an interest in keeping those waters safe," Justin said, "and have authorized their navy to escort merchant vessels. For a price, of course. Much as I hate to put myself at the mercy of extortionist colonials, they *have* formed a squadron to patrol the West Indies, and our safety lies with them. We will proceed with our plans to return to Florida, and while I'm there I will meet with the American officials and see what is being done about this situation, and about getting escorts back onto the open seas and away from the pirate nests."

Peter looked at his friend's face, and suppressed a tingle running down his spine. He did not want to be a pirate at the receiving end of that look.

"We should have expected this. Since the war's end, all those out of work privateers have to do something with themselves. We can't keep risking cargoes and lives, though, without taking steps." Peter paused. "Do you think it's safe to take Suzanne on this trip to Florida?"

"I wish I could say it's safe, but sea travel is always a risk. Most ships get through without incident, and if we delay until we can get a convoy together—" He stopped and grimaced. "We cannot delay. And frankly, Peter, at this point I would rather face pirates than Suzanne if I tell her she's being denied this excursion she's anticipated for so long."

"Don't worry, Justin. This may have been a fluke. After all, Ryan was a captain who had a less than stellar career with Delerue. I have a great deal more confidence in your other captains."

"I hope you are right, Peter, for all our sakes."

Peter excused himself and Justin walked up to his room to prepare for supper. He was to attend a card party this evening at the home of Mrs. Fanshawe, a local widow with an eye toward advancing herself socially by snagging Lord Smithton, either as a generous lover or, in her avaricious dreams, a husband.

Justin was not a green boy and was aware of her machinations, but his friends and family had been encouraging him to get out more, and it wasn't the worst way to pass an evening. Nevertheless, he expected to sleep in his own bed tonight. The widow's overblown and obvious charms left him cool.

As he was shaved by his valet, he eyed himself in the mirror and thought to himself, as he often did, *Where is Christine? What is happening in her life? How does she keep herself?*

The mirror offered no answers. It never did.

* * *

"I am bored, Mr. Davies, B-O-R-E-D. You promised me a life of excitement, and so far piracy has been voyages cruising point-to-point, broken by brief moments of terror."

Julius raised his eyebrows at her where she lounged against the starboard rail.

"Terror for our victims, of course."

"Of course," he murmured. He returned to looking out to sea with her spyglass, and suddenly chuckled deep in his throat.

"You have the magic touch, Captain Daniels," he said, and passed her the glass.

Christine pushed herself off the rail and focused on the brig bearing down through the Florida Straits. As the figurehead came into focus, she saw it was a carving of a winged creature with the petulant face of a woman who bore a disturbing resemblance to the vicar's wife.

"The *Harpy*," she murmured. "Damned convenient, if you ask me, Smithton naming all his ships for mythological creatures. It does make them easier to spot.

"Remind me to send him a letter of thanks," she said, giving him back the glass.

The mate took it and they silently studied the ship sailing to America. The *Tigress* had put in at Key Marquez for water and was now headed north to Fernandina. It would be a fine thing, Christine remarked aloud, if they had some salable goods in their hold when they got there.

"Of course, they're likely headed to Fernandina as well, so we'll have to make sure we arrive well ahead of them. Mr. Davies, be so good as to call Gunner Goose up on deck."

Gunner, whom Christine was pleased to note was within days of having taken his monthly bath, stomped across deck followed by Sally.

"Gunner, that ship is carrying too much canvas. Can you relieve her of some of that weight?"

Gunner grunted, and eyed the ship.

"Sylvestre! Hawkins! Get your arses over here and bring a match!"

Gunner looked at the distance, the roll of the waves, the wind, and grunted again.

"With luck, two shots, Cap'n."

"Gunner, you do it in two shots and there's a bonus for you in Spanish dollars. And extra corn for Sally."

"Aye, Cap'n. Stand back, Sally," he said lovingly.

The goose waddled away to safety. With the speed and skill of years of piracy, the men opened the gunport and prepared the 12-pounder.

"It's too far." Julius crossed his arms over his chest. "He won't make it with that light a gun."

"I have a gold piece that says he does it in two shots, Mr. Davies."

"You're on, Captain," the mate said. The rest of the crew was gathering 'round to place their own bets, while the crew of the *Harpy* responded to the sight of the *Tigress's* open gunports with a flurry of activity of their own.

Gunner blew the match and waited for the downward roll, then touched off his cannon and sent a ball screaming over to splash harmlessly into the Atlantic.

"Hold up, Mr. Howe."

Chris took the speaking horn from Davies.

"Ahoy the *Harpy*! Surrender now, or we will resume firing!"

For answer the *Harpy* opened up and fired from two port guns at the *Tigress,* but their gunner had neither the skill nor range of the *Tigress.*

"Speed and cunning," she murmured to herself as Gunner fired again while the *Harpy's* crew reloaded. "Well, well, it looks like Sally's going to be a well-fed goose this evening." Christine grinned as the foremast came down in a tangle of canvas and lines. "Bring us in, Mr. Davies."

"Aye, Captain," Julius said, bellowing orders to the *Tigress's* crew. When the *Tigress* came up alongside the damaged *Harpy* and made fast, Christine grabbed a line at the call of "Boarders away!" and swung over with the crew, but the *Harpy's* men had little fight in them once the officers were forced to surrender. The merchantmen were required to carry guns to purchase insurance, but arriving at port alive was more important to the sailors than arriving with a full hold.

"Fetch the doctor," Christine called back to the ship. Two of the *Harpy's* men suffered broken arms from the falling yards and there were cuts and bruises all around, but thankfully, no loss of life. The ship had recently put in at a West Indies port and the squawk of caged chickens and ducks added to the general confusion, and the pirate crew helped themselves to the fresh provisions, ferrying them over to their own ship.

Julius returned to her side.

"The hold's well stocked. A search of the captain's cabin failed to turn up any documents or strongboxes."

"Goodness," Chris murmured, brought back to the moment. "If I were a suspicious person, I'd wonder about that. Fetch the captain here, Mr. Davies."

Two of the *Tigress's* men hustled the captain forward, a pistol placed at his back.

"This booty is all very good, Captain Ralston, but I also want your correspondence for Delerue Shipping's Florida offices."

Captain Ralston, his weathered face confused, blurted out, "Our correspondence? Why?"

"Dear me, am I the one at the wrong end of the pistol? You are to answer my questions if you wish to be able to sail back to England."

"There is no correspondence," Ralston said, recovering himself.

"Really? Imagine, if you will, my disbelief, Captain."

Ralston's lips set in a stubborn line, and he said nothing.

Christine sighed dramatically and said, "It seems you *will* to be awkward about this, Captain. I am sorry, you leave me no choice. Secure the captain and crew below, all of them except for…that one," she said, gesturing at a panicked sailor whose face drained of color when he was grabbed by Cooper and Hawkins.

As the crew was chivied below under the guns and eyes of the *Tigress's* crew, Julius came alongside his captain.

"Let me guess. You have a cunning plan..."

"I need to know where those papers are, and I am not about to spend all day tearing the ship apart to find them. I can get the information we want, and enhance Christopher Daniels's reputation as the scourge of Delerue Shipping in the bargain.

"Get Robin up here, and tell him to bring his knives."

"What are they going to do to Simmons?"

Clifton, the mate, spoke in an undertone to Weaver. The two had shipped out with Ralston before, and knew he wouldn't easily give up Lord Smithton's papers.

"Maybe they think Simmons knows where the capta—"

Weaver's words were cut off by a blood chilling scream from abovedecks. All the *Harpy's* crew froze, while their guards stood by, impassively.

"Was that *Simmons?* My God, he screamed like a woman!"

The hatch opened and a pirate silently came down the ladder. He held a bloody knife in his hand, and after looking over the silent crew, pointed it at Weaver.

"You."

Weaver was hustled to his feet and brought blinking into the sunshine. The pirate captain, Daniels, stood next to the windlass in his coat of vivid satin that shimmered like a field of daffodils in the tropical light, the exaggerated shoulders giving him a triangulated body. He stood with a cutlass at his side and Weaver's knees nearly gave out when he saw the red gore dripping from it. His captors gripped him and frog-marched him through a gauntlet of silent pirates, each holding a reddened blade.

They halted in front of the captain. The clothes were those of a fop, but there was nothing languid in the intense brown eyes that studied the prisoner.

"You are the purser, Weaver."

Weaver's throat was too tight to speak, and he jerkily nodded.

"I have a problem, Mr. Weaver. I hoped Mr. Simmons would tell us where your captain keeps what we want. Alas, he was full of lies and we had to…dispose of him. Perhaps you have more accurate information to share with me?"

Weaver didn't know where the captain hid his papers, but he knew it was worth his life to guess, and he did, babbling out everything he knew or suspected about the captain's hiding places.

Captain Daniels listened impassively, then said, "That is helpful, Mr. Weaver, but I don't believe it is helpful enough. Sadly, I no longer have a use for your services."

He nodded to the pirates holding Weaver, and within moments he'd met the same fate as the hapless Simmons.

The darkened hold echoed with Weaver's scream, abruptly cut off. One man's lips moved in less than silent prayer, and the smell of fear made the dank air ripe. The hatch opened again and the same pirate came down the ladder. This time the blood was smeared up his arm to shoulder height. He looked around the hold, then brought his gaze to rest on Clifton.

"You."

"No!"

Captain Ralston jumped to his feet and pushed himself forward, brought up cold by two blades blocking his path.

"Don't take any more of my men! I will tell your captain what he wants to know."

The pirate snarled, "Up with you then," and Ralston's hands were cut loose so he could climb the ladder.

The deck was awash with fresh blood and the captain walked through the silent pirate gauntlet until he was eye-to-eye with his adversary.

"The bulkhead behind my bunk has a false panel. What you seek is there."

With a flick of his eyes, Captain Daniels signaled to his men, and after some hammering and the sound of wood being torn asunder in the captain's cabin, they returned carrying a strongbox.

The crew broke into cheers, cut off at a wave of their leader's hand.

"Thank you, Captain Ralston. Now you shall learn what happened to Simmons and Weaver."

"Wha— But I gave you what you wanted!"

Captain Daniels just nodded, and the pirates grabbed Ralston and marched him past the bloodstained deck to a cabin. The hatch was flung open, and inside, bound and gagged on the bunk, sat Weaver and Simmons looking furious and frightened, respectively.

Ralston stared at the "dead" men.

"But—the blood!"

"Ah, yes, the blood," said the husky voice of Captain Daniels, coming up behind him. Ralston turned and looked at the handsome pirate. "Our cook was so enamored of the thought of fresh poultry in the galley that he got carried away when he saw your chickens. I apologize for any confusion it may have caused."

Ralston turned purple, then white as the pirates' laughter rang out around him.

"Don't take it too harshly, Captain," said Daniels with a gleam of real sympathy in his eyes. "Your employer knows it is all part of the cost of doing business in the West Indies."

Ralston's curses filled the air as Christine exited the cabin, and her men cheered again when she came abovedecks.

"Good screaming, Robin."

"Thank you, sir," Robin touched his forehead with one bloodied hand, then looked at the sacrificed chickens at his feet. "I have a new dish I've been wanting to try out in the galley, and these should do nicely for it. Maybe I'll call it 'Buccaneer Surprise.'"

"I look forward to testing your recipe personally, Robin, and I'll leave you in charge of these beauties," Christine said cheerfully.

When she was back in her cabin, she paced while waiting for Julius to return with a hammer and chisel, and with the right tools he had the hasp open in a trice. It was better than she'd hoped, full of gold and letters from Smithton to his factor in St. Augustine regarding the disbursement of monies and goods.

"Almost enough here to spread among the men and send them on their way," Chris said, running the coins through her fingers. "We have been beyond fortunate so far, Julius, but I can't keep risking men's lives for gold."

"They want to risk their lives for gold, Captain, it's their nature."

"I understand that, I am the one responsible for their lives. I am the captain. And it is one thing to risk the lives of my men, but what of Smithton's people? They don't deserve to pay for his sins."

She tapped the letter in front of her.

"He's coming back to Florida, Jules. It's going to be our last haul."

"And then?"

"Let's take care of meeting Smithton," Chris said, "Plenty of time after that to deal with 'and then.'"

While Julius counted the loot, Chris read her husband's letters, annoyed that she felt more guilt at reading another person's correspondence than she did at robbing him. Smithton's letters informed the factor the earl himself would be arriving soon on the *Phoenix*, accompanied by the earl's sister, Lady Suzanne Delerue, and Peter Marlowe.

"I am also hopeful," the letter said, "that upon my arrival you might present me with some news of my beloved wife, Christine Sanders Delerue, Lady Smithton. I am most anxious for any word of her well-being, and pray you will meet me with information."

Christine traced the words with her finger. "Beloved wife," she mouthed silently. She knew it didn't mean anything. It was the kind of language one used in correspondence. But there was a part of her that wondered what it would be like if someone said the words truthfully. She had dreams at night, sometimes. Confusing dreams that woke her, gasping for air, as if she'd run a long distance. Justin Delerue was in those dreams, a different Justin. A Justin who held her and kissed her and looked at her with love. She heard the men of the crew pairing off, and she saw them together in the tight quarters of the ship. They found companionship in the dark, brought together by danger and lust, friendship and need. Hell, even Gunner had Sally. There was no one here she could be close to, other than Julius. And that wasn't what she wanted, not anymore.

She frowned at the letter in her hand. It was time to exorcise the demons troubling her dreams.

Chapter 9

The *Phoenix* had fair winds to Florida. It was the lull between winter and the hurricane season, and the crew and the ship's owner were grateful for smooth sailing. Justin stood at the rail staring to the west, and Peter Marlowe sighed silently as he joined his friend. It didn't take a gypsy mind reader to guess what Justin was thinking.

"Perhaps there will be word waiting for you. We may even intercept the *Harpy* and hear something before landfall."

Justin turned away from the sea, his green eyes shadowed. "It's been a year, Peter, and I have heard nothing. It's as if she fell off the face of the earth." The large hand resting on the rail tensed for a moment. "Or was swallowed by the sea."

"Are we in sight of Florida yet?" Suzanne joined the men, her small face alight with excitement beneath the chip straw bonnet the wind tugged away from her chestnut curls. Lady Suzanne Delerue wasn't considered a great beauty, but her open ways and sunny personality brought animation to her face, and her older brother watched over her with a fond, if vigilant, eye. He'd seen the way Peter looked at her now that she'd left the schoolroom and was pleased by the thought of his best friend forming an attachment for his sister. Suzanne could look higher for a spouse, but Justin didn't believe she could do better. After his own disastrous marriage, it was important to Smithton to see his sister settled with a man who loved and cared for her.

"Where's Mrs. Dawkins?"

"Oh, she's below repacking some of her things. I'm going to miss having her as my companion when she returns to her family."

"Perhaps you won't need a companion for much longer, my dear," Justin said, enjoying Peter's discomfiture. Watching the two of them pretend there was nothing between them had been an additional entertainment during the trip.

"Mrs. Dawkins says some believe a Spaniard discovered the Fountain of Youth in Florida," Suzanne said, deftly steering the conversation to sightseeing plans. "Imagine the fortune you could make, Justin, if you were able to ship that elixir back to England!"

"I can think of many ladies of the ton, and gentlemen too, who would pay dearly for a rejuvenat—"

The call "Sail ho!" interrupted Peter, and Justin shaded his eyes with his hand, looking across the water from the ship's stern while Peter and Suzanne speculated over the identity of the approaching vessel. It was a welcome diversion from the tedium of their safe, boring journey from England. Captain Smathers was at the taffrail, glass to his eye. The strange ship was cutting through the Atlantic waters, coming up fast on the port side.

"It looks to be a Venezuelan vessel, milor—wait a moment, they're lowering their flag."

By this time, the silent passengers could see with their own eyes the flag lowered and replaced a moment later by a black banner with a white tiger's head.

"Pirates!" Smathers yelled, shouting to his crew to unfurl every inch of canvas. The pirate schooner was bearing down rapidly, its gunports open, the crew sanding the deck for action.

"Take Suzanne below with Mrs. Dawkins," Justin shouted to Peter above the din. "Bring back the weapons in my locker!"

"Justin, I'm scared," his sister whispered. He gave her a reassuring smile and squeezed her hand, hard. Over her head, the two men's glances locked—Suzanne's fate at the hands of pirates wasn't to be contemplated. Peter broke away and took her gently by the elbow.

"Come, my dear. It will be safer for you below. You can help us best by reassuring the Widow Dawkins that all will be well. You know by now your brother and I have been through worse scrapes than this."

Captain Smathers, a veteran of too many pirate skirmishes, knew the schooner gaining on the heavily-loaded merchantman was outsailing them. He was joined at the stern by Justin.

"Can we outrun them?"

Smathers grimaced and ran a hand over his glistening pate. The pursuing vessel was now close enough they could clearly see the figurehead of a snarling tiger on its bow.

"I don't think so, milord. Whoever is sailing that vessel knows what he's doing, and I would have to wager he knows these waters. Even if we could put more distance between us, we might find ourselves on a reef."

The two ships were within one hundred yards of each other when the *Tigress* fired a warning shot from the bow gun. A massive bald man with a heavy gold earring stood at her starboard bow and raised a horn. "Heave to, *Phoeni*x! Allow us to board and no one gets hurt!"

"What assurances for our safety?" Smathers shouted back. There was a pause while the pirate bent, conferring with a man in black who was adjusting the ruffles at his wrist. The giant straightened. "Captain Daniels of the *Tigress* gives you his word as a gentleman."

Justin's eyes narrowed at the pirate's effrontery. This was the same Captain Daniels who had taken the *Manticore*. No gentleman he, but more likely some jumped-up salt who'd knifed his superior for control of the ship. Smathers cursed roundly. "I don't see any alternative, milord, but to allow them to board. I don't know who this Daniels bastard is and he's got us at his mercy. If we give them what they want, we may scrape through."

Justin nodded grimly. "I know him, Captain. He's already hit the *Manticore*, but he didn't kill the crew. We are going to have to take him at his word." Suzanne's safety came first. Nothing else—not his pride or his cargo or even his own life was as important as that.

The pirates cheered when the *Phoenix* hove to, keeping their guns aimed broadside at the British vessel. Longboats from the *Tigress* rowed over as a half dozen pirates swarmed the rigging to keep their muskets trained on the *Phoenix's* decks. Within a short period armed men clambered aboard, the grinning giant followed by the lithe, slender pirate Captain dressed in black, a rakish red silk bandana on his head and red silk shrouding his lower face.

The mask was a good sign, Justin thought. The scum must be planning on letting them leave and didn't want to be identified later. If the pirate had exposed himself, he might have to dispose of witnesses.

Chris swallowed as she scrambled over the rail. She'd brought her coolest, most trustworthy crew members. At all costs she hoped to avoid any bloodshed between the two vessels. She peeked at her husband under her lashes. Justin Delerue was bigger than she'd remembered and he still looked very much like the man in her dreams. He affected an air of disdain as he stood aside from the commotion, arms crossed over his broad chest, but she could see a muscle twitching at his jaw. Standing so close to him and her goal of freedom made her anxious as well, and she clasped her hands at the base of her spine so no one would see them shake, legs apart in a stance she trusted looked insouciant, yet commanding.

She peeked at her husband again. Yes, that was the look, aware of everything, yet above the fray. It seemed to come naturally to *him*, but she was getting better at it. She mentally braced herself with that thought as Julius took a position at her right, and they waited for Cooper, Robin, and the others to join them. Her crew rounded up the *Phoenix's* sailors and efficiently checked for weapons before herding them together under guard. A tense silence settled over the deck and Christine scanned the faces arrayed round her before saying to Julius in a low voice, "This isn't all of them, Mr. Davies. Search below again."

Julius in turn barked her orders to find any remaining passengers and crew and bring them on deck. When the party emerged from belowdecks, Cooper held a struggling young woman by the upper arm. Robin followed, wringing his hands in dismay as a stout older woman in black bombazine berated him for being "a pusillanimous villain who would think nothing of ravaging helpless women!"

"Now, now, ma'am, please don't carry on so. I'm sure Captain Daniels doesn't intend to hurt you. He's really a nice man, not at all the sort to molest a lady!"

Cooper snorted in disgust and Christine rolled her eyes with a sigh. Robin was a talented cook, but he'd never make a good pirate.

"Get your hands off her, you scum!"

Peter Marlowe broke away from his guard, grabbing a pistol from a startled Robin's belt. Christine took it all in at a glance and was running across the short space separating them as Robin wrestled with Marlowe for the gun. There was a sharp report and a flame lanced across Christine's shoulder, spinning her back and nearly knocking her off her feet. She recovered in time to see Silvestre and Howe grab Marlowe, disarming him. They shoved him roughly toward Suzanne and Justin.

"Don't hurt him!" Chris drew in deep breaths, the red scarf fluttering, then turned her anger on Marlowe. "You stupid, buggerin' sod! Are you trying to get people killed?"

Julius rushed to her side, but she waved him back and pulled a handkerchief from her sleeve, holding it against her wounded arm. "I'm all right. Start unloading the cargo—I do not want to be here any longer than necessary. Cooper, Silvestre, dammit, keep them under guard! Robin, go below and fetch some water for the lady."

Mrs. Dawkins, normally the most stouthearted of ladies, had fainted dead away when Howe grinned at her. Christine turned to her captives. Peter and Suzanne had enough sense to look terrified. Justin, now that his sister was out of danger, had again affected an air of polite boredom. Christine scowled behind her mask. She was sweating like a pig in the tropical heat, her silk mask was plastered to her face, and her arm burned as if seared with a hot poker while Justin Delerue, Earl

Smithton, was determined not to let a bunch of scurvy pirates make him show fear! She wondered what it would take to upset his sangfroid.

A sudden, manic grin slashed across her face. She shut down the little voice in her head that screamed what she was thinking was very, very stupid.

"It seems my guns aren't enough to convince you not to try anything foolish," Captain Daniels said in a raspy voice. "I believe having one of you as our 'guest' will keep the others in line."

Suzanne inched closer to Peter, who put his arm around her shoulder. Chris rested her dark gaze on her sister-in-law, her eyes narrowed. Justin took a half step forward, fists clenched, brought up short by a cutlass prodding his midsection. Not so sanguine after all.

Christine bowed in Suzanne's direction. "Don't worry, my dear, you're not whom I had in mind."

Peter whitened and moved closer to Suzanne. Chris winked at him.

"Don't you worry either, darlin'," Her eyes shifted back and she smiled behind her scarf. "I will take *that* one," she said, languidly waving her bloodstained lace handkerchief at her husband. "The tall, sultry one with the burning eyes."

"Oh, bloody hell," Julius muttered behind her. "This isn't a robbery, it's a French farce!"

"Shut *up,* Mr. Davies!" Chris said under her breath. She sighed dramatically as her crew began to leer and poke one another. "A leisurely cruise through the Caribbean sounds heavenly. Moonlit nights, soft sands, good food—careful with that case of wine, Howe! Yes, that is just what I need. Some rest and...relaxation. Mr. Cooper, keep order while I take my guest to the *Tigress.*"

Justin, Peter, and Suzanne began protesting as one.

"Silence!" roared Julius, before he leaned down and whispered fiercely in her ear, "Have you lost your bloody mind?" Christine ignored him. Justin Delerue wasn't the only one on this deck with poise.

"Oh yes, please don't do anything foolish, gentlemen, to put this young lady at risk," she drawled. "Mr. Marlowe, Lady Suzanne, you may continue your journey. Smithton will stay with us to guarantee your safe passage. I would *so* hate to get into a battle with civilians about. All that noise and mess." She shuddered delicately and let Julius tie the handkerchief around her reddened arm until Brown could look at it. The look Julius was giving her spoke volumes, but he didn't contradict her in front of the crew.

* * *

Justin Delerue stood silently, hands clenched at his sides. Suzanne's safety was all that mattered. Nothing they could do to him—he felt sweat trickle down his back, unseen—was as important as Suzanne. Orders were given for his personal belongings to be fetched from his cabin and he felt a twinge of optimism. Perhaps the scum would slip up and include his razor or gun case.

"Take our guest aboard the *Tigress*, men, and secure him in my cabin. Don't damage him!" Captain Daniels said, turning from where he watched the cargo being transferred to give Justin another look that made his blood cold. "He's gently bred and a prime article, boys, and isn't used to your games."

Rough hands grabbed Justin and dragged him across the deck as Suzanne cried out and Peter held her back from running to her brother. For Suzanne's sake, he didn't resist as the pirates tied his hands in front of him and keeping a firm grip, hustled him into the longboat. He sat silently as they rowed to the *Tigress,* the pirates comparing notes on what they'd do with their shares of the loot. When they reached Daniel's cabin, the tone of their jests changed and Justin began to struggle in earnest despite his bound hands and his good intentions.

"Tie him up good, boys!"

"Face up or face down?"

Hawkins chortled. "Ye know the gentry, they likes to talk first! Let's leave him face up! If the Cap'n needs help, he'll call us."

Silvestre made a low whistling sound through the gap in his teeth. "Ain't he a big 'un? 'Bout time the Cap'n had some fun too!"

"Think we should cut his duds offa him?"

"Naw, Cap'n may want to do that hisself. He's mighty handy w' that pigsticker a' his."

This last sally brought new guffaws from the crew. In short work, they had him lashed spread-eagled to the oversized bunk. They admired their handiwork, each knot properly shipshape to secure him. Hawkins sighed and straightened the bandana on his oily locks. "Wish someone'd do that for me."

"Later, m'dear," Powell said, patting him on the arm. With a few more rude jests, they went above, Silvestre shutting the hatch with a wink and a blown kiss for Justin.

* * *

Suzanne trembled in Peter's arms as the pirates continued transferring gear. They'd been pushed into her cabin along with Mrs. Dawkins while Robin, his weapon back in his possession, kept watch outside the hatch.

"Oh, Peter, what's going to happen to Justin?" Suzanne wailed.

"Hush," he whispered, then squeezed her, hard. "Don't worry about your brother, my dear, he's capable of taking care of himself. Believe me, knowing you are out of danger will help the most."

Peter's brow furrowed as he listened to the pirates laughing and talking on the sunwashed deck above. It had just occurred to him the pirate captain had referred to all of them by name—even knowing Suzanne's given name. And he knew their destination. There was something more going on here than he could figure out, but that would have to wait until he had Suzanne safely ashore.

Chapter 10

The cabin hatch closed firmly behind the pirate captain. Justin stopped testing the strength of the ropes and glared at the tall, masked figure leaning one padded shoulder against the hatch. The pirate's red cravat was looking wilted, the black satin shirt and coat torn and darkened by blood. Justin noted the damage with satisfaction, even as a frisson of fear ran down his spine. He couldn't ignore what he'd seen abovedecks and the lewd comments of the men who'd bound him to the bunk, but he knew better than to reveal his anxiety.

"Lay one hand on me, sodomite, and there won't be a hole deep enough for you to hide in!" he snarled.

The captain's eyes crinkled at the corners. The blackguard was smiling behind his mask! Captain Daniels's slow glance raked the earl's lean body, bound hand and foot to the bunk. The gaze lingered on Justin's broad shoulders, sliding down past his flat belly to his firmly muscled thighs. The pirate's eyes rose back to meet the earl's and didn't look away as a slender gloved hand unwrapped the red silk scarf.

"You!" Justin gasped.

Captain Daniels smiled, a smile not reflected in her gleaming brown eyes.

"Spare me your dramatics, my lord. The only thing I want from you is a divorce."

Justin stared at his wife, speechless, as she sauntered across the cabin to perch on the side of the bunk. Conflicting emotions battled within him. Relief that Christine was indeed alive, and rage at discovering she was the pirate who'd been harassing him and robbing his ships.

Her mouth quirked up at the corner. "I must indeed be changed if my own husband doesn't recognize me."

Rage won.

"YOUR HUS—"

A leather gloved hand covered his mouth. She leaned over him, so close he could see the gold flecks in her eyes. "Don't make me gag you, Smithton. To my crew, I am Captain *Christopher Daniels*, and the consequences will be most unpleasant if they hear you bellowing about being my husband." She cautiously raised her hand a few inches.

"Maybe I'll shout it to all and sundry and end your little farce!" he sneered.

"I do not think so." The corner of her mouth twitched again. "For one thing, I could cut your throat before going abovedecks to deal with whatever issues arise." His eyes widened at her matter-of-fact tone. "And I am willing to risk that you'd rather have people think you were captured for ransom by the notorious pirate Daniels than held up by your own wife. One story makes you an unwilling victim, the other leaves you a laughingstock."

"'Captain Daniels?' You ran away from me and I drove myself ragged searching for you! I thought you had drowned! I planted a garden in your memory at Rosemoor and now I find, all this time, you have been playing pirate!"

"I haven't been playing pirate, I *am* a pirate," she said in aggrieved tones. "Unless you agree taking back my own money is justice and not piracy."

"I won't carry on a conversation while bound to your bed! Untie me at once!"

She snorted, rolling her eyes toward the ceiling. "I am a pirate, not a lunatic. If I untie you now, I strongly suspect you'll leap up and throttle me!"

Since that was exactly what Justin had in mind, he could only snarl and tug uselessly at the ropes. "Throttling you would only be the beginning, madam!"

Christine studied her gloved hand.

"A man tied hand and foot to my bunk is threatening me with mayhem. I am aquiver with dread." She looked at him from under her lashes and settled herself more solidly into the bunk, resting her hand on his chest. "It's been a while since I have had a prisoner tied to my bunk. The last one was special. He was so skilled and eager to please."

That shut him up. She sighed.

"A pirate's life is not all fun and rum, you know. Especially for the captain. The nights can be lonely for those who command. Maybe if you demonstrated the proper enthusiasm, I might be persuaded to make your stay less...restrictive, Smithton."

"You can't keep me here!"

He tried to say it forcefully, but it came out a bit higher pitched than he would have liked.

"You would rather bunk with the crew? Certainly, if you prefer. But consider this, Smithton. In *my* cabin, you only have to suffer *one* pirate's attention."

The hand resting on his chest was stroking him, her black-gloved knuckles tracing a line between his nipples. Justin stared at his wife, eyes wide. This went far beyond anything he could imagine in either his worst nightmares or his wildest fantasies. She seemed totally absorbed in the contrast of her black leather glove to the fine white lawn of his shirt. He cleared his throat.

"Madam, I cannot carry on a reasonable conversation while tied this way."

"Hmmmm?"

"Untie me, Christine." He swallowed. "Please."

She stopped stroking him and looked startled, a light flush coloring her cheeks. "Right," she said, pulling back from him and tugging her jacket into place. "I'll consider letting you up because we have issues to resolve between us, but first I need your parole."

"My *what?*"

"Lower your voice, dammit." She was completely serious now. "I want your word if I untie you, you will not try to harm me or any member of my crew, or attempt to damage my ship. You will not get back to the *Phoenix*, and if I am going to let you run tame, I have to know I can trust you not to sabotage the *Tigress*."

Justin lay still, fuming silently until he realized she meant it. Either he gave his word or he'd find himself bound to her bunk for the duration of the voyage while facing, maybe not a fate worse than death, but a fate he didn't want to think about at the moment.

"Very well," he gritted out. "I give you my word. Now let me up! Please," he added when she just looked at him.

Christine unhurriedly reached down to her boot, withdrew a dagger ,and began sawing at the ropes. She leaned across Justin to undo his left hand and her bound breasts brushed across his chest. He turned his head away, but not before he'd inhaled her fragrance, an aroma of jasmine and sandalwood. She unbound his other hand and pushed herself off the bunk. When he sat up to work at the ropes on his feet, she held out the dagger, hilt first, her gaze steady upon his. He looked at her a moment before taking the weapon. He lowered his eyes to the ropes and, in silence, finished the job and swung his legs to the deck. He held the razored blade for a few heartbeats longer, then reversing the dagger, handed it back to his wife.

Justin looked at her closely from head to toe, pursing his lips at the padding in the front of her trousers. "You don't seem to be much like the girl I married."

"That girl doesn't exist any longer. She has been replaced by Christopher Daniels. For now, anyway."

"To find you, after all this time." He looked at her as he rubbed his wrists. "What does all this mean, Christine—your running away, the piracy?"

She backed away from him and, swinging a chair around, sat astride it, putting distance and a solid chair back between them as they talked. He was startled at the masculine gesture, but it seemed in keeping with her demeanor. His wife had taken on all the aspects of a young man, had immersed herself in a role so deeply that he could see how she could fool her own crew and his into believing she was indeed Christopher Daniels.

She took a deep breath. "I ran away from you, Smithton, because I was frightened. I robbed you because I was angry. In both instances, my goal was the same—freedom. I want to be free to live my own life and I need a portion of my dowry back to do that. Now that you know I am alive, you can return to England and petition Parliament for a divorce. I don't care what you say about Christine Sanders, she doesn't exist anymore and won't reappear. Tell them I ran off with another man, or that I'm a criminal, or that I was unbearable to live with, I don't care. Your divorce will be recognized in the United States as well, and you'll be free to find a wife more suited to your needs. You have enough of my money left that you don't need *me* any more and we can end this farce once and for all."

Justin cocked his head and stared at her, puzzled. "This is about *money?* I would have given you money. You would have a generous allowance to buy yourself whatever you like, Christine. Don't you think I would take care of my wife?"

She smiled sadly and shook her head. "You don't understand. You'd be giving me back *my* money."

"Your money, my money—it's *our* money, Christine. We are married!"

"In the eyes of the law, here and in England, it became *your* money when you married me, Smithton. You know that. You could dole it out to me if you want for pin money, but there were no provisions in our marriage for me to keep anything. If my father had been alive to negotiate on my behalf, it would have been different. I'm sure my uncle made no plans for my dowries to be handled for my future welfare. The marriage contract is what you expected and what the law allowed." She looked at him. "Be honest. Did you think I would need money stashed away in Devonshire while 'breeding up a race of giants'?"

His cheeks blushed dark red and shame washed through him. "You heard us in the library. I'm sor—"

"Don't apologize! I'm *glad* I heard you and Marlowe! Far better I should go into married life knowing what you expected than to be disillusioned later." The corners of her mouth tilted up. "Things have improved in my life recently. I've got my money now. The *Phoenix* was not the first ship of yours I've visited."

"Yes, I heard about the *Manticore*," he said, frowning.

"Um, only the *Manticore*?"

"What othe—the *Harpy*?" He sucked in a horrified breath. "You robbed the *Harpy* too?"

"Just so. That is how I knew you were coming back to Florida."

"My God," he said, running his hand through his hair. "Was anyone hurt?"

She seemed surprised at his concern. "No, no one was hurt. Well, a few scrapes, but no loss of life. We tricked them and were able to get what we needed with a minimum of fuss."

"You could have been shot...your arm! You were hit when Peter's gun discharged!" He reached to take her arm and she pulled away from him, keeping the chair back between them like a shield.

"Not to worry, Dr. Brown already saw to it while you were being escorted to my cabin."

She rubbed at her wounded arm and Justin frowned at the gesture. "Is it bad?"

Christine dropped her hand. "It hurts, but it isn't unbearable. After all," she smiled, "we pirates have to expect a wound or two as the cost of doing business. And speaking of business..." She took a deep breath. "I understand Sanders Shipping cannot be mine, but now I have enough to make a life for myself." She shifted her gaze to the floor then back up to him.

"You need a wife who will be the kind of countess you've always expected, someone who will fit into your world and be your helpmate. I think we both know I'm not that woman."

All the nights at Rosemoor he'd wallowed in guilt came back to him and he looked away, unable to face her.

"I treated you poorly from the first, Christine. Our wedding night...I'm sorry for that. You deserved better. Damn, any woman deserved better than the clumsy treatment you received." He looked back at her, his green gaze intent as he surprised her in a blush. "I wasn't trying to be intentionally cruel. And, as you know, I was drugged." He paused. "I've had over a year to regret we couldn't have started differently."

Christine sighed. "I don't know you well enough to judge if you're a cruel person."

He winced as her dart struck home.

"I do know I was coerced into what, for you, was simply a marriage of convenience. That is not what I want from life, and that is not what I want in a husband." Her eyes narrowed. "Why haven't you had me declared dead and looked for a new wife?"

He stood and turned from her to look out the porthole. Above him were the sounds of the *Tigress's* sailors at their tasks.

"I've asked myself that question many nights and, to be honest, I don't have a good answer. I would like to think it was because there was always a belief inside me you were still alive, that I wasn't responsible for driving you to your death. As long as I was still bound to you, there was hope you were alive." He watched a fat gull swooping for its dinner. "But I'm not sure any longer if that is the truth. Maybe it was my pride—I hate to be bested and it was as if the sea had snatched away what belonged to me.

"And now," he said swinging back toward her, "I would like to know why you have kidnapped me and what your plans are."

"At the moment, my plan is to change out of these bloody clothes and return abovedeck. Please turn your back."

"Oh, I don't think so," Justin drawled, leaning against the bulkhead and crossing his arms. He might be her prisoner, and he had given his parole, that did not mean he had to jump to her tune in everything. "Afraid I'll uncover all your secrets? Surely someone who runs around a ship full of men and ties prisoners to her bunk cannot be shy?"

Christine frowned at him. Clearly she hadn't considered all the ramifications of having her husband in her cabin, even for a short stay. Then she shrugged, wincing at the pull on her bandaged arm. "As you wish. Enjoy yourself."

She turned her back on him, gingerly slipped off her coat, and began unbuttoning her shirt.

"Do you need help?"

She paused, and looked at him over her shoulder, seeming to gauge the seriousness of the question.

"No, I can manage. Thank you."

She turned back to her task and Justin studied her, catching her glance as she looked up and saw his reflection in her mirror as her shirt slipped off. Christine's back and shoulders were muscled, not rounded like the women he was used to seeing unclothed. White bindings constricted her breasts, matching the bandage on her upper arm. She didn't remove her breeches, denying him the opportunity to study the rest of her, but the changes since they first met were obvious. Even disguised he could appreciate her sleek, feminine form. She reached into the chest for a fresh shirt, carefully pulling it over the bindings on her chest and arm and doing up the buttons. The waistcoat followed and she tucked the shirt into her breeches. A coat finished the ensemble. Pomade was rubbed between her hands, then slicked through her tousled curls, smoothing them close to her head. She splashed water into the basin and wiped her face and neck, then smeared a small amount of ash above her lip for an afternoon "shadow." A fresh cravat was tied 'round her neck in an elaborate knot that would have made Rogers weep with envy. She again raised her eyes to the mirror, then turned, spreading her hands wide.

"Behold, Captain Christopher Daniels, at your service, milord."

"Quite a performance, madam," he drawled, clapping his hands slowly. "If I didn't know for a fact what was beneath the bindings and padding, I would be quite convinced I was standing here with a young man."

She inclined her head in acknowledgment and reached for a wide brimmed straw hat hanging next to the mirror. She adjusted it and examined herself in the glass. The black trousers were a nice contrast to the buttercup satin waistcoat, and the bottle green coat complimented the ensemble. The fop in the glass was ready for the afternoon. She adjusted the lace at her wrists, then turned to her husband.

"We need to work out the details for ending this marriage in a manner satisfactory to both of us, Smithton. You will be my guest for a few days until we reach a safe harbor. There you can make arrangements to return to St. Augustine and meet up with your sister and Peter Marlowe."

Justin's hands clenched. "I don't want Suzanne dragged into this."

Her gaze slid away from his. "It's too late. I didn't want to do it this way, but I have to believe there's less chance of your men trying something heroic to retrieve you and the money if I keep you close to hand. Now I suggest you make yourself comfortable. We had your personal effects brought from the *Phoenix*, and forgive me for having them searched, but we thought it best to remove your pistols."

There was a knock at the hatch.

"Cap'n? Beggin' your pardon, but you're needed above. Mr. Davies's cabin's ready for your guest," Robin said.

"Thank you, Mr. Robin, I'll be there in a trice. Please stand by to escort our guest to his quarters." Captain Daniels turned back to Justin, her brown eyes twinkling. "You will be staying next door in the mate's cabin, where you will be undisturbed. You are welcome to use the day room and come above."

"We're not sharing your cabin?"

"Despite my earlier claims, I don't make it a habit to have my wicked way with attractive prisoners. And don't worry about my crew," she chuckled as she stepped out the hatch, "they know you are the captain's prize and not to be molested."

Captain Daniels inclined her head to her guest and exited, her husky laugh floating behind her.

Chapter 11

Justin followed the young sailor with cherubic gold curls across the day room to his quarters, a cabin mirroring Captain Daniels's in size and furnishings. It was neat and well appointed. He diligently searched the small desk, but found no logs, manifests, or journals that would give him information about the *Tigress's* activities. All personal possessions were gone, replaced by Justin's own belongings. After using his brushes and the looking glass, he paused in the hatchway leading topside, bracing himself for the coming ordeal, the knowing sniggers of the pirate crew.

It was somewhat anticlimactic to find the crew busy at their tasks and for the most part scrupulously avoiding looking at him as he walked to the rail and stared out over the empty sea. A faint noise disturbed his reverie. A large goose eyed the tassel on his boot as if it were a particularly tasty barnyard bug. Justin gave the bird the "Smithton stare" that had managed to quell any number of encroaching mushrooms and importunate mamas of marriageable chits in London, but the goose was made of sterner stuff. She bobbled her head and hissed at him.

"I wouldn't make eyes at Sally," rumbled a deep voice. "Gunner is a jealous man and a dead shot."

Justin stiffened, recognizing the large lout who had backed up Christine. He turned the same freezing gaze on the pirate. It didn't faze him either.

"I don't believe we have been formally introduced." He grinned. "I'm Julius Davies, Chris's godfather and mate of the *Tigress.* No doubt you've heard about me from that rodent Beachum. And you must be Chris's…umm, Justin," he said, glancing over his shoulder to make sure there were no eavesdroppers. "I have heard much about you. I trust you found everything satisfactory in the cabin?"

"There are less comfortable prison cells. I suppose I should be grateful I wasn't tossed over the side by *Captain Daniels's* gallant crew."

Without waiting for an invitation, Julius leaned his bulk against the rail alongside the thin-lipped earl, gently nudging Sally away from temptation. "And wouldn't that be a terrible waste of good tailoring,"

Davies said, examining the body sporting the products of London's finest craftsmen. "No, Captain Daniels is more careful than that with our booty, as are the men. Aye, quite a captain, our Chris. Amazing how this crew and ship have come about in a short time."

"You will forgive me if I do not applaud your captain's accomplishments."

"Oh, I didn't come to seek compliments. I *know* how hard the captain's worked to get to this point. Daniel Sanders would give the captain an awful scolding if he was here, but mayhap he'd be proud too."

"Daniel Sanders...Christopher Daniels...of course," Justin murmured. "I should have seen it."

"Yes, they were quite close, Daniel and the captain. Your father, Charles, would have also liked our Chris, I'm thinking."

Startled, Justin gave Julius his full attention. "You knew my father?"

"Oh, aye. While your father was visiting America, the four of us—Daniel, Charles, myself, and Anne, Chris's mother—were inseparable. That's why your fathers were so anxious to see you two together."

Justin had a hard time imagining his cold and formal father relaxing with a colonial merchant, his wife, and a half-breed pirate. Charles Delerue never spoke with his son about his trips to Florida. Their relationship hadn't fostered sharing confidences over the evening port.

"Hard to believe they're all gone now," Davies said, clearing his throat gruffly. "But you are here, and so is Chris."

"You make it sound like we are on a honeymoon," Justin said bitterly. "I would hardly call this a pleasure cruise. Were you the one who encouraged this mad start of hers, Davies? I thought she was dead, not playing pirate!"

Davies looked at him levelly. "Captain Daniels is not playing pirate," he rumbled. "Captain Daniels *is* a pirate. And a damned good one! There's not a man jack here who would not sign on for another voyage with Chris and the *Tigress.* They'll leave this ship wealthier than when they arrived and in one piece for the most part. Not many captains can say they've done as well for their crews!"

The big man gazed off at the horizon. "Life's opportunities are what you make of 'em, Smithton. Captain Daniels learned that lesson. Who knows but *you* may undergo a sea change into 'something rich and strange' during your time aboard the *Tigress.*"

Justin's hands clenched on the railing. Unless he jumped over the side, he'd be aboard ship for the foreseeable future, and it would be best to be prepared. Good preparation included knowledge of one's enemies.

"Tell me of my wife, Davies."

Julius slanted him an unreadable glance and checked again to see that they were alone. Christine was across the ship, examining a gun with Howe. "Well, now, there's much she should be telling you herself, but I can share with you a bit about the girl. You've already met her bastard of an uncle and I'll hope you're bright enough to figure out he was only after the girl's money."

"Why didn't she simply say no when he raised the issue of marriage?"

"Beachum could have made her life hell on earth had he chosen to. She had to go along with his wishes."

"She should have told me! I would have helped her get away from him!"

Davies looked at him steadily. "Would you? Would you help a young woman you didn't know leave her lawful guardian?"

Justin opened his mouth to reply, then frowned it shut. "She should have trusted me once we were married."

"Why? She didn't know you well enough to trust you."

The earl shifted uneasily, Davies's words echoing Christine's.

"So," Julius said evenly, "here we have a young woman raised as her father's heir, only to discover she's being manipulated into a marriage with a stranger who doesn't want her, just her money. Betrayed by her uncle, betrayed by a beloved father who didn't make adequate provision for her future, no one to turn to but an old sailor hiding from polite society. Not a situation likely to inspire confidence, is it? *I* applaud her. This was all her idea, she was the one did the training and planning and execution. I know few men, and fewer women, who could have turned their lives around that way. Now the question is, do you want to be rid of your wife of convenience?"

"Isn't that what you want for her, to be rid of me? Based on what she said to me earlier, I believe my absence from her life—as long as she has her money—would make her quite happy."

"I want her to be safe and content. Happiness would be a bonus. One final thing, Smithton." The big pirate smiled gently. "A ship is a dangerous place. If Chris comes to harm while you are about, you will wish you'd never left England."

Justin looked at him steadily. "I'm gratified she had a safe haven and a protector to turn to, but whatever happens now must be worked out between my wife and myself."

Davies stared at him a moment longer, then chuckled. "I wish you luck working things out, Smithton. Good day. Silvestre! Fake down those lines and look smart now!"

Justin brooded and watched the busy ship's activities. The crew were a rough lot, but not much different than the crews of his merchantmen. The *Tigress* itself was a trim ship, well cared for, and the crew seemed content. When Peter and Suzanne landed in St. Augustine they'd report Justin's kidnapping to the authorities, but if what Christine said was true, he'd likely be on his way back to the city before a rescue could be mounted.

He put his hands behind his back and walked around the deck. He spied his wife talking with Davies, and Justin stood for a moment watching her. If the crew took their inspiration from the captain's disposition, it was no wonder they were content. Christine seemed to glow, and clearly had the respect of her crew. She strode the deck in perfect rhythm with the sway and roll of the ship and he studied her masculine disguise at his leisure. As he noted in the cabin, she'd done a good job of making herself over as a young man. He stared at her bosom, recalling well how substantial she'd been the last time he saw her. She must have bound herself tightly to achieve her new look. He felt a stirring in his groin as he imagined slowly unwrapping her and freeing those bountiful treasures. Back at Rosemoor when he'd imagined himself reunited with his runaway bride, the daydreams were all of grateful glances and sedate embraces. His fantasies about bed romps had never included his wife, but now she was here, and he was here, and neither one of them was in a position to be playing the roles society expected of them.

Christine looked up from her papers and caught Justin staring. Even from a distance, he could see the color staining her cheekbones when she realized where his gaze was centered. She turned her back and continued with her work. A slow grin spread over his face. So the dreaded pirate who ties men to her bunk blushes. Perhaps this voyage could be more entertaining than he'd thought. A "sea change," indeed!

Christine watched Justin approach and braced herself for who knew what. She was already regretting the impulsive kidnapping. It would have been much simpler and wiser to take the money, run, and write him a letter saying, "Dear Lord Smithton. I am still alive. Please give me a divorce. Sincerely, Christine Sanders."

He came and stood next to her, too close. "You have a fine ship here, *Captain Daniels.* Has it been in your possession long or did you recently steal it?"

"Save your sneers. I didn't steal the *Tigress.* She's been in my...family...for some time. When I go stealing, Smithton, I go after more portable goods. And people."

"Yes, I didn't ask you about my ransom. Will it be costly for me to say adieu?"

"You might say your fee was paid in advance with cargo, Smith—"

"Justin."

"I beg your pardon?"

"Call me Justin. If your crew thinks what I believe they are thinking, you might as well refer to me in more intimate terms. And may I call you...Christopher?"

"I prefer you address me as 'Captain' or 'Captain Daniels.' Too much informality aboard ship can lead to difficulties."

"Ah, well, I wouldn't want to contribute to a breakdown of discipline. But I insist you call me Justin."

She sighed. "Very well, Justin. What can I do for you?"

"I thought that, since I was your guest, you'd take time from your schedule to talk with me and perhaps stroll around the deck. I'd like to know what you have been doing since we last spoke. Other than robbing Delerue Shipping, of course."

She pulled her hat lower over her eyes and chewed her lip. It *was* her fault Justin was here, and it wouldn't hurt to be nice to him for a few days. If she maintained cordial relations with him, he might be more inclined to see her point of view regarding the divorce and speed the process.

The crew had things well in hand and they were making good time along the coast. Even if Justin were familiar with Florida's shoreline, he'd have a hard time determining their destination. She took Julius aside about keeping the charts away from Smithton, then rejoined her husband. She was aware of the glances they received from her crew, but none of the men seemed to take her cordiality toward their prisoner amiss. If anything, they seemed glad their captain had improved his social life. They had an astounding amount of sentiment, for pirates.

As she and Justin strolled, she told him in a low voice about her year with Julius. "…then I went out to retrieve the fish and this large raccoon was sitting there, eating my dinner and scolding me for disturbing her!"

Justin laughed and her heart skipped a beat. For a moment, she could only stare, his sardonic face transformed. *Oh my,* she thought, *Julius was right. Kidnapping Smithton was really, really stupid.* She mentally shook herself and concentrated on what he was asking, something about fishing in the rivers.

"Oh, aye, the fishing is good in these parts, though you do have to be careful of snakes and alligators."

"Alligators? I've never had the opportunity to see the fearsome lizards, but I understand they are quite common."

"They are, and when we put in to shore, you might hear them roar in the evenings. They can be hunted for meat too, and are quite tasty, but hard to kill."

"Cap'n Daniels!"

Christine looked up, answering the hail from the bow.

"When you've got a moment, we have a question about our heading," Davies said. She excused herself and strode away, but she could feel Justin's eyes on her as she left him.

Toward the end of day the ship dropped anchor in a secluded cove and a party was sent ashore for fresh water. The men cheered when the landing party returned with the water and an unexpected bonus, a small wild pig. Soon a fire was laid in the sand and the sweet smell of roast pork filled the air. The crew celebrated its bloodless heist as Caribbean pirates had for centuries, dancing, feasting, and dicing in the sand. They good-naturedly thanked the earl for his bounty and Christine thought he bore their jests with surprising grace considering their differences in status—not to mention their redistributing his goods. He sat in the sand alongside them, his fine clothes and boots scratched and stained as he ate roast pig from the bone with his fingers, just as they did, and drank from battered tankards that never went dry.

"A toast!" Gunner said, Sally safely cradled at his side. "A toast to Cap'n Christopher Daniels, the luckiest and fairest captain to sail the Florida straits!"

"To Cap'n Daniels!" roared the crew. Christine blushed in the darkness and stood, waiting for the raucous cheers to die down. She cleared her throat.

"Any success I have had I owe to the crew of the *Tigress.* You are the finest men I've ever known, each and every one of you. With our work today, we are ready to return to homeport and retire the *Tigress.*" She grinned. "But if I ever find myself short of funds again, I'll know whom to call.

"And now," she said, raising her hands as the crew cheered again, "I'm for my bunk and dreams of a quiet retirement." She motioned to Justin and he raised his brows, but rose to his feet and dusted himself off, obediently falling in alongside his captor. They walked a few yards in silence to the shore. At the edge of the water, a boat was beached and the *Tigress* floated in the moonlight, a ghostly galleon in the tropical night.

"We'll wait a bit for Richard and Robin and we'll all row back to—hello, what's this?" She crouched down in the sand and began brushing at it, gloves busy in the soft light. Justin watched her, puzzled, when suddenly she laughed, a delighted, girlish sound, and pointed.

"Look, turtles! They are coming out of their eggs!"

She scrambled back and held out her arm to block him from coming too close. "Watch now! They will head for the ocean!"

Sure enough, within a few moments, a small, dark form had dug its way out of the hole and slowly, laboriously, began dragging itself by its flippers to the water's edge. Christine watched in wonder as first one, then another, and another baby loggerhead began its timeless journey to the warm sea. Not all made it. A sharp-eyed comorant snatched up one before it could make it to the relative safety of the water. But most of its nest mates made the journey safely. One, distracted by the distant glow of the pirate's fire, headed in the wrong direction. Christine gently picked it up and carried it to the water's edge where the hatchling found its bearings and headed out to sea.

"Is that not marvelous?" Her face was aglow. "I didn't expect to see turtles this early in the summer."

He looked into her shining eyes and something within his chest shifted, slightly. Behind them, Justin could hear the music the men played on their pipes and fiddles.

"Dance with me, Christine."

She stared at him and retreated a step. "What? Dance?" Her eyes narrowed. "Why?"

"Because there is moonlight. Because there is music. Because there are turtles." He smiled, his teeth as white as the light reflecting off the water. "Because we have never danced together. You do dance, don't you?"

"Aye. I mean, yes, I enjoy dancing. Are you sur—"

"Listen! We can waltz to this melody. Have you ever waltzed?"

She slowly shook her head, still watching him, trying to figure out what he was up to. But when he held out his hand, she took it, and he peeled off her glove so they were flesh to flesh. The shock of feeling his heat against her bare skin almost made her retreat, but he grasped her securely. With his other hand, he removed her hat and laid it in the sand. Then, still looking into her eyes, he pulled her close and began the waltz. It was difficult and certainly different, Justin thought, waltzing with someone in trousers and boots. It also had advantages. Christine brought the same grace she showed on deck to the dance, partnering him as no other had. Without skirts, he could feel the length of her leg pressed against him. He could shift his hand on her lower back and press her hips close to his and, if he couldn't feel the beating of her heart through her coat and bindings, he could see in her eyes that she wasn't unaffected by the moment. Together they drifted across the moonlit shore, two tall silhouettes against the water and the night.

Christine was afraid to speak, for this dancing on the hard sand was nothing like the cotillions of her youth. She'd never been partnered by someone who wasn't intimidated by her size, but Justin treated her as if she were tiny and precious as he held her, guiding her through the steps. She could smell him, a mixture of bay rum and a scent that she'd recognized in the cabin as uniquely his. She breathed deep and unconsciously moved closer. They said nothing, but listened to the faraway melody. When the music stopped they stood a moment, looking into each other's eyes, until a hail from Robin made Christine jump back, nearly losing her balance. Justin's hand shot out and, without thinking, he grabbed her wounded arm. Christine yelped and pulled away.

"I'm so sorry!" Justin was appalled. "I forgot about your injury!"

She cautiously rotated her arm. "I'm sure you didn't mean harm, Smithton. It is a good reminder for me to take care." She rubbed at the bandage. He said nothing as they joined Richard and Robin at the boats pulled up on the beach, and they rowed back to Robin's chatter about the beach celebration. He was still silent as Christine proceeded him down to his cabin.

"I will bid you good night, Smithton, and see you in the morning." She turned toward her own cabin.

"A moment," he said, glancing up and down the empty corridor.

"Yes?"

"It is customary for husbands and wives to exchange a kiss when they say good night."

She licked her lips, her mouth gone dry. "After everything that's happened today, that hardly seems wise if we're soon to be permanently parted."

"If you only did what was wise, you wouldn't find yourself in the position you are in today," he said, the corners of his own lips quirking up. "Come now, surely a captain of such renown isn't afraid of a kiss?"

"Buggerin' sod," she said under her breath, then, "I am not afraid to kiss you!" He just smiled and moved closer. Christine locked her knees to keep from taking an involuntary step back against the bulkhead, and a small shiver ran down her spine when her husband put both hands alongside her head and leaned forward, slowly, stopping only when his lips were a fraction from hers. She tensed, hands fisted at her side. "What are you wait—"

Whatever she'd started to ask was lost as he swooped onto her opened lips, his arms coming around her, pinning her to his long, muscled length. He was even then careful of the wound in her arm, or perhaps he'd wanted to rest his hands on her hips all along. Too startled at first to register all that was happening, Christine stood still as her husband explored her mouth. The sensation was strange, yet somehow seemed familiar. Then she moaned as realization flowed through her, along with a growing warmth. This was what had brought her awake from her vivid dreams, gasping for air. Waves of sensation, pouring over her, engulfing her and robbing her of her senses. He pulled from her what she did not know had been lurking inside, waiting for this moment. She felt caught like a fly she'd seen in a pitcher plant in the woods—lured by the sweetness, but once inside it was doomed. She felt she was drowning in sugar syrup and pushed against Justin's chest. He released her mouth, but held her for a moment longer. He was having trouble with his own breathing.

"Enough, Justin. Let me go," she said in a low voice.

He sighed and stepped back from his wife. "I don't suppose I can persuade you to step into this cabin and continue our conversation?"

"N-no. It is my fault you are here, but I'll not compound my error with further foolishness."

His brows lowered at her dismissal of his embrace. She brushed a strand of hair back from her face, trying to regain her composure. "It *is* exceedingly foolish, for I still intend to terminate this mismatched marriage, Smithton."

"Back to Smithton now?"

"It is best we keep a bit of distance between us. As I said earlier, informality aboard ship can lead to problems." She took a deep breath. "I will see you in the morning, Smithton."

"Justin, Christine. My name is Justin." He paused and his voice softened. "If we are only going to spend a short time together, let us not put artificial barriers between us." He reached to smooth the curl falling across her forehead, but she retreated, reaching behind her to swing the hatch open.

"Good night. Justin."

He brushed past her, and she was aware of every inch of his body that touched hers in the narrow corridor. As she leaned to close the hatch, he put his hand on top of hers.

"You'll tend to your arm before retiring?"

At her curt nod, he smiled. "Excellent. I am counting on you to return me to St. Augustine safe and sound. Good night, Captain. Sweet dreams."

She frowned and turned down the corridor to her cabin, idly rubbing her sore arm. She didn't look over her shoulder, and she knew he watched her retreating back.

Justin didn't see her again until luncheon. He couldn't be sure she was avoiding him because he made her nervous, but the thought was still pleasing. The morning was spent quietly writing in his journal, reading, and observing the ship's routine. The Florida coastline was empty of all signs of civilization, only the passing ships in the distant sea-lanes reminding him he was not alone out here on the water. The weather continued fair and at luncheon Davies mentioned hurricane season wasn't far off.

"By the time the storms hit, we will be in safe anchorage," Christine offered.

Justin said nothing, listening carefully, hopeful she'd let something slip about her plans for the future. Instead, the conversation shifted to the daily routine of the *Tigress.*

"The men have weevil races scheduled for tonight, Cap'n."

"Mmmm. Keep an eye on Silvestre, Jules. He lost a lot of loot last time and wasn't happy about it."

"Weevil races?" Justin asked.

Christine grinned. "They're monstrous entertaining. I've seen horses with less spirit than some of the little buggers. I hear tell Howe has been grooming his entrant for days."

"If anyone understands the workings of a weevil's mind, it would be Howe," Davies said.

Justin winced. He wasn't prepared for a wife who enjoyed racing vermin and sprinkled her conversation with raw language, but he'd deal with one crisis at a time.

"And what are your plans for this afternoon, Chr-Captain?"

Christine looked at her husband and sipped her ale. "We'll drop anchor later and drill the crew. Maybe get some weapons practice, time permitting."

"Weapons? Perhaps I can participate. I'm not used to sitting idle."

"Really?" She arched her brows. "I thought you British lords sat around your clubs all day playing cards or visiting your tailor."

"Some do, but that is not how I spend my time."

She looked interested, so he went on. "Like you, I was raised to work in shipping. It was my older brother who was the heir to the title. I was only the spare," he said.

"What happened to your brother?"

"Roger died in a riding accident." Justin swallowed at the memory of his father's shattered look as they put his firstborn son in the family crypt. "By that point I was already living in London working at Delerue. My family has never shirked from dirtying our hands at increasing our holdings. That, no doubt, is what brought my father to Florida originally—business with Sanders Shipping."

"I never met your father, Smithton, but mine spoke often of their friendship," Christine said. "And you knew the late earl, didn't you, Julius?"

The large man grunted his assent while he studied the maps. A pair of spectacles was perched at the end of his nose, an incongruous sight with the jaunty red bandana tied 'round his head and the gold loop winking at his ear.

"Good man, Smithton," he rumbled. "Handy with his fives."

"I remember," Justin smiled, "he gave me boxing lessons when I was a lad. Said it would stand me in better stead for going away to school than all the Latin I could learn." His smile faded and he gazed off into the distance, thrumming his fingers lightly on the table. He didn't often remember those times when he and his father had been close. "That was before my mother died. He was right too, about needing some skill at fisticuffs at school."

He shook himself, brought back to the present. "So what say you, Captain? Does my parole include trusting me with a weapon amongst your crew?"

Christine blew out a breath.

"Just try not to get yourself killed. It would be difficult to ship you back to England for burial."

He grinned at her. "My dear Captain, I am trusting you to keep your prisoner safe and sound and returned in one piece, as promised. The crew assured me last night that Captain Daniels is a man of his word."

Davies and Howe put the crew through their paces that afternoon while Christine observed with a critical eye. Justin stripped down to shirt and trousers, paired with Cooper for swordplay, and the two circled each other, watching eyes and hands for subtle signals.

Christine watched the earl as he watched Cooper. She had been concerned about him being injured. The rolling deck of a schooner is not a fencing *salle* and Cooper came from a rough school of fighting, the one that said a match is won when you're still standing and your opponent isn't.

Cooper's reach was longer, but Justin had more bulk, and he handled his cutlass like someone used to a blade, and Christine relaxed a fraction. The crew gave the match to Cooper, but barely, and Cooper himself added a rare "Well done" at the end. Christine rubbed her shoulder reflectively. After her wound healed, it might be interesting to match her own blade against Justin's.

As the sun began to slide into the west the men put up their weapons, secured the guns and, stripping off their clothes, went over the side for a swim. Justin hesitated briefly, but after wiping the sweat off his forehead shrugged off his own clothes and dived off the side, slicing cleanly into the sparkling waters. He swam parallel to shore with smooth strokes, then turned and made for a sandbar some yards in toward land where the crewmen were lounging. He stood in the shallow seas, back to the *Tigress*, hands sluicing the water from his ebony hair. His broad shoulders and corded back tapered to a trim waist and chiseled hips, long legs gleaming in the afternoon sun. He walked up on the sandbar, the muscles clenching in his bu—

"Here. You look overheated."

Christine squawked, fumbling not to drop her spyglass over the rail. Julius stood beside her, holding out a tumbler of water.

"Thank you," she said. She looked at the cup in her hand, dashed it into her face, then passed it back.

"That isn't what I mea—what *are* you staring at?"

"Nothing!" She slammed the brass tube shut, her cheekbones glowing crimson. "Just keeping an eye open for sharks. Can't be too careful in these waters!"

Julius just sighed, took the spyglass from her limp hand, opened it and focused on the swimmers. "Let us see, there's Silvestre's hairy arse, and Howe and...merciful heavens!" Julius gave a low whistle and paused, adjusting the glass. "Now *there's* a sight to set a maiden's heart aflutter. Are you sure you want to throw this one back, Chris? I've seen worse. Usually in my own bed."

Christine started to speak, cleared her throat, wiped her face, and tried again.

"Well, he's pleasant enough to look at, I suppose."

Julius stared down at her and lowered the glass.

She tossed her hands in the air. "Right. Go ahead, you have been dying to tell me how foolish I was to bring him aboard! Have your say!"

"My dear child, this is the most entertainment I've had in months! I can hardly wait to see the next act!"

"Buggerin' sod." She scowled and stomped off to her cabin.

"Too true, child, too true," he murmured, refocusing the glass.

Chapter 12

Robin outdid himself that night preparing supper. Conch soup, fresh poached redfish with lime sauce, the *Tigress's* own "Buccaneer Surprise" chickens, which Smithton praised while everyone delicately refrained from explaining the dish's origin, hot biscuits, a salad of greens and citrus, ginger cakes and fine wines courtesy of the swag from the *Phoenix*. The talk was lively as Julius, Richard, Christine, and Doctor Brown discussed the future of the Florida territory. Justin mostly listened, every now and then interjecting his opinion as an Englishman.

"You watch, Captain Daniels," Dr. Brown said, poking his fork at the captain for emphasis, "Andrew Jackson is going to do his best to make Florida the southern tip of the United States."

"He's going to have plenty of opposition. Remember what Mr. Randolph said in the American House of Representatives? 'No man would immigrate into Florida—no, not from Hell itself!' There's a lot of strong feeling in Washington against a land full of swamps, frogs, Seminoles, and gators! The idea of full statehood for Florida is farfetched, Doctor," Christine replied. "Jackson's already talking about returning to Tennessee, though I'll grant you, he's managed to do much already. But our laws are a hodgepodge of English and Spanish custom, and it's going to take Moses rather than Jackson to straighten them out."

"Is that the same Jackson who fought at New Orleans?" Justin asked.

"Aye," said Cooper.

Smithton waited for him to expound further, but he just sat there. No one else was surprised, and Christine made another attempt to draw the carpenter into the idea of social discourse.

"You were at New Orleans with Jackson, weren't you, Cooper?"

"Aye."

"And?"

The man looked at his captain with a jaundiced eye. "New Orleans was hot, bloody, and French."

Christine knew when to admit defeat, and turned back to Brown who said, "Ceremonies transferring Florida to the United States were held in both St. Augustine and Pensacola. Imagine what it will do to St. Augustine if Pensacola becomes the capitol! Could seriously affect your business interests, Smithton."

"What about the southern part of the peninsula?" Justin asked. "Is that arable land?"

Davies shook his head. "Southern part's only fit for mosquitoes and Indians. The land's mostly swamp and the Keys are infested with wreckers and pirates."

"Shocking, that," Justin remarked, straight-faced.

"Indeed," Davies agreed without a hint of irony. "The *Maria Louisa* was taken not long back and the rascals made off with over forty thousand in loot. There's no one down there who can clear out the pirates."

"Forty thousand dollars?" Christine said, awe in her voice. Justin shot her a fierce frown and she quickly added, "Terrible, just terrible. Was anyone hurt?"

"Fortunately, no," Davies said. "I do hear, though, that the crew and passengers were terrorized. The pirates threatened the supercargo, stripped him of all his clothes, and were going to hang him off the mizzen yard."

"Any idea who it might have been?"

"There's talk it was a nasty Spaniard named Ramirez, recently seen in Cuba. Sound familiar, Captain?"

"Imagine that," Christine leaned back in her chair, fingering the dirk at her side. "Senor Ramirez gone from terrorizing defenseless whores to terrorizing entire ships. I should have gutted him when I had him under the knife in Havana."

She and Julius both ignored the stunned look on Smithton's face and Julius said, "Let that be a lesson to you, Captain. No good deed goes unpunished."

When dinner was done, Christine dabbed at her mouth and sent for the cook.

"That was delightful, Robin." She smiled at the young man nervously twisting his spotless apron into knots. "Even our guest praised your work. Is that not so, Smithton?"

Justin opened his mouth and seemed about to make a snide comment, maybe about his purloined wine, but when he looked at the cook's face, it was obvious it would have been too much like kicking a puppy.

"It was a fine meal, Robin. Far better than I have had aboard any of my own ships."

"Oh, thank you, sir!" Robin beamed. "Y'see, it's the datil peppers—a bit of that in the sauce with the fi—"

"Enough. Back to the galley," Cooper gruffly said, taking Robin's arm to escort him out. Christine could tell from the lightening of the carpenter's features he enjoyed hearing his protégé praised by their fine guest. Cooper had confessed to her once in a rare moment of conversation his dream of having his own inn. With Robin as cook, their success seemed assured. Chris absently rubbed at her bandaged arm.

"Leave that wound alone, Cap'n," said Brown. "You don't want it to get inflamed."

"It is nothing. Just a scratch."

"I've see people lose limbs in the tropics from what started as just a scratch. You let me know if that wound worsens."

"Yes, yes, I will," she said irritably, reaching for the rum bottle as Brown and Julius excused themselves for their nightly chess match. She poured herself another measure of rum, ignoring Justin's frown.

"Do you always drink this much or is it a reaction to my being here?"

A smile raised the corner of her mouth. "I thought it was wives who nagged their husbands about drinking, not the other way around. Relax, Smit—Justin, it's been a long and tiring day."

She did look fatigued, and a bit flushed, but she had her coat on in the warm cabin, and her cravat high around her neck. His eyes lingered on her as his brain conjured images of her looking sleepy and rosy in her bunk, freed of the confining men's clothing. He couldn't get over the changes in Christine's appearance. An extremely striking woman had been inside the spots and excess weight.

Her self-assurance added to her attractiveness, but it also complicated matters. It wasn't that he wanted her to be so poor-spirited and desperate that she would throw herself into the safety of the marriage without regard to her feelings, or his, but it would solve a number of problems right now if she did not feel so sure of her ability to fend for herself.

And if she wasn't so confident she did not need to be married to him. Justin swirled the rum in his own glass.

"How long do you plan to keep me here?"

"It will take us a few days to come about to our next stop where we'll put in for fresh water. You will be left near enough to a town to hire transportation."

"Do you like roses, Christine?"

She stopped rubbing her arm and considered the unexpected question. "I like roses, but they don't do well in St. Augustine. Too much heat and moisture, I'm told."

"England is perfect for roses. There are roses blooming now, at Rosemoor. When the windows are ajar their scent perfumes the house. The earl's suite in particular is fragrant with vines planted by my ancestors."

"For fragrance our Florida jasmine is much prized. It wouldn't do well, transplanted to a less hospitable climate."

Justin arched an eyebrow, acknowledging his wife's point. He leaned forward and began tracing circles on the table near where one slender hand rested. In the privacy of her cabin, with only her husband, it wasn't necessary for Captain Daniels to hide the smallness of her hands.

The gloves were off.

Christine watched the long, tanned finger making wet circles, and took a fortifying sip of her rum. It did nothing to cool her off, but it helped steady her as her husband went on in that rich, cultured voice that made her want to lean in closer to be sure she heard every word. But she knew better, and stayed still in her seat.

"Florida *is* beautiful, Christine, but sometimes it is nice to be somewhere else, a place where you can watch the seasons change. In the spring in Devon, the daffodils thrust up through the ground, reaching for the sun, growing and swelling in the light."

She looked down at the table, mesmerized by the finger that had left off stroking the table and was now lightly stroking the back of her hand. Every nerve in her body seemed focused on that one, small spot.

"In the summer the crops ripen and all is lush and green. It can get hot, but when the heat seems unbearable, a quick plunge into the pond in the home woods can leave you feeling refreshed. Just lying there and letting the water stroke over your body can be most rewarding."

Her hand was now being slowly stroked, turned so those long fingers could access her supple wrist. Her pulse leapt beneath him as he caressed her. She wanted to say something, anything, but no words came to mind as the images he conjured and the sensations he produced flowed over her like soft water.

"Autumn is also special. The harvest comes in and all at Rosemoor gather together to celebrate. The cider is tart and spicy, and we dance till late under the moon. It is pagan, I know, but many of these old customs are holdovers from when the farmers took fertility rituals to heart. Do you know," he said solemnly as he continued stroking her wrist, "once upon a time, the lord of the manor was expected to play a role in these rituals and prove his abil—well, never mind that."

Christine swallowed and tried not to think about pagan rituals.

"Ah, but winter may be my favorite season. You might think otherwise, imagining it as a time of chill and darkness. When I was a child, my family would travel to Northumberland to visit family at the holidays. In winter, there's nothing finer than being tight and snug inside..." Her pulse took a funny jump again beneath his warm fingers. "...watching the snow fall past the windows."

"Um, what's it like?"

Justin looked her directly in the eye.

"I beg your pardon?" he said softly.

"Snow! What's snow like? I have never seen it, y'see, only read about it."

He was still looking at her and holding her hand. His pupils darkened and filled his eyes.

"Some things cannot be described. They can only be experienced."

He tugged gently on her wrist, pulling her forward across the table. She braced herself with her free hand, but didn't resist as he tugged her toward him, still watching her eyes. Her lashes fluttered down at the same moment his lips grazed the corner of her mouth. Startled, she turned her head away and Justin took advantage of the motion to brush his lips across her cheek until they were next to her ear.

"Come with me. Let me show you things you've never experienced."

Whatever Christine might have said was lost in the knocking at the closed hatch.

"Cap'n? Dr. Brown's sent round a posset to help you sleep tonight."

Awareness flooded back into Christine along with a heated blush. She hastily pulled away and, for a moment, mentally damned Dr. Brown and the entire crew. She cleared her throat, rising from the table. "I'll be right out, Robin. Lord Smithton and I are done here."

Justin was still watching her steadily as he rose to his feet. If she hadn't seen the leap of the pulse at his throat, she'd have thought him unaffected.

"I'll bid you good night, Justin. In the morning, we'll talk some more."

* * *

Justin was tossing in the dark on Davies's wide bunk. Alone. The hatch creaked open, a large shadow filling the doorway.

"Smithton? You awake?"

"What is it, Davies?"

"It's Chris. Her arm's inflamed and she's running a fever. We could be in for a long night."

"I'll be right there." He pulled on trousers and shirt, hurrying after the mate to the captain's cabin. Inside, Dr. Brown was trying to coax Christine into drinking something, but she kept shaking her head.

"Come along, Captain, it will help you rest."

Christine tossed her head and pushed the doctor away. Davies sat down on the bunk next to the patient.

"Now, Chris, listen to the doctor. He knows what's best for you."

"Uncle Julius?"

"Yes, poppet, I'm here. Drink now, and we'll have a nice chat."

She swore under her breath and took the cup, grasping it with shaking hands. She shuddered at the taste, but drank it down. Her face was flushed and her teeth chattered. She was wearing a man's nightshirt, now untied at the neck and slipping off her injured arm. Brown glanced over his shoulder and saw Justin standing just inside the cabin.

"What's he doing here?"

"It's all right," said Davies. "Smithton is her husband."

Brown raised his brows.

"Someday, Julius, I'd like to hear the whole story." He looked at the earl. "The captain's wound is inflamed. I'm going to take another look at it, and it may be ugly. Are you staying, Smithton?"

"I'll stay," Justin said grimly. "Tell me what to do."

Brown grunted. "Julius, let Smithton sit on the bunk. Now, Captain, I'm going to unwrap your bandage. Smithton, it would help if you'd hold her."

"He doesn't have to hold me!" Christine cried out. Her eyes were bright and she looked dazed, and ready to weep.

"Yes, I know, you have got bigger ones than Julius, but I'm the doctor, so do as I say, dammit!"

Justin sat beside his wife, awkwardly wrapping his arms around her midsection. He was nervous about jarring her injured shoulder, but firmly put his hand on her forearm to keep her from shifting. Brown dispassionately undid the remaining nightshirt ties and pushed the garment down to her waist. He unwrapped the wound and Justin's breath hissed from between his teeth when he saw the angry-looking flesh. Christine clutched his arm, panting, her fingers digging into his flesh, and she turned her face into his shoulder and moaned as Brown washed the injury and re-bandaged it. Justin wanted to do something, anything, to ease her, but at least the doctor was competent and worked quickly. Justin eased her nightshirt back in place and retied it, then helped his trembling wife scoot back under the covers.

Brown sighed as he gathered his tools. "She'll have a nasty scar, but it's better than losing an arm. Julius, I don't want her alone tonight."

"She won't be," Justin said firmly. "I'll spend the night here."

He glared at Davies, but the other man just lifted his brows.

"Fine with me. I'm needed at the helm with Chris out of action."

"Doesn't anyone want to know what I want?" asked a raspy voice from under the covers.

"No!" all three males chorused.

Brown set a small bottle on the table, alongside a pitcher of water. "Laudanum. Try to get it down her if she wakes, along with as much water as she'll drink. I'll bleed her tomorrow if it becomes necessary.

"Captain, my orders to you are to sleep as much as you can. That will help your body speed the healing process. Good night, Smithton."

Justin absently thanked the doctor and turned down the lanterns so that only a glow of light remained in the quiet cabin. He settled himself into the chair beside the bunk for a long night, listening as his wife's raspy breathing evened out into slumber.

"Hot, Papa, 's hot here..."

Justin jerked awake. Christine thrashed in the bunk, her face flushed, but dry. He dampened a cloth and sat beside her, wiping her brow.

"Papa?"

"Shhh...It's all right. It's Justin. Here, try to drink a bit of water."

"Justin! Don' tell Justin! He'll take it away."

"Hush, Christine, no one's going to hurt you. You're ill and not in your right head."

"No, Justin...Don't tell."

Justin sat on the bunk beside the fevered woman and carefully slipped his arm beneath her, lifting her shoulders for a drink. Heat radiated from her body and, when he took the cup away, she fretfully plucked at her nightshirt.

"Hot...So hot."

He was afraid she'd hurt herself thrashing about, but if she were cooler she might rest. He dampened the cloth again and untied her shirt, pulling the two sections apart, and began gently sponging her down. His knuckles grazed the underside of her breast and he swallowed, concentrating on smoothing the cloth over her fevered flesh and not being distracted by her plump, rose-tipped breasts. They were smaller than he remembered from their wedding night, but still full and rounded. He rewet the cloth and brought it low, down her belly and across her ribs to her tapered waist. Christine's body had been lushly attractive on their wedding night, now her beauty was sharper, honed by hours of swordplay. It was the difference between an overblown rose and the smaller, hardy jasmine.

"Snow...wan' snow."

She was mumbling again and he spoke to her in a low, soothing voice, barely aware of what he was saying.

"We'll have snow, sweetheart, we'll go home to Rosemoor and there'll be snow." He continued to freshen the cloth with the cooling water and wipe her down, speaking soothing nonsense, but she was beginning to thrash again. He climbed into the wide bunk beside her, anchoring her body with his leg thrown across hers.

"Hush, Christine, stay still. It's Justin. Shh…don't fuss, I won't hurt you."

"Justin? Mus' leave Justin, hide. Justin took everything. Head hurts."

She whimpered softly and he tightened his grip, holding her close. He looked down at the fevered woman, all alone except for an old sailor, a ship full of pirates, and a husband she feared. Driven by feelings he couldn't explain, he leaned forward and kissed her on the forehead. She was still hot.

"Justin?"

"Yes, Christine, I'm here."

She smiled and opened her eyes, glittering and unfocused with drugs and fever.

"Not naked." She giggled. "Look nicer naked."

"Thank you, I think," he said dryly. "You also. Now try to sleep, sweetheart."

"No' swee'heart. Don' wan' to be a wife."

"I know, you've told me."

"Wan' to be a mistress."

He looked down into his wife's face, and she was looking at a point somewhere past his shoulder and smiling.

"A mistress. Wear pretty clothes, dance with Justi'. See him naked," she said dreamily.

"Christine, you may see me naked any time you like."

"Waltz naked?"

He swore. That fast, he was hard as a pikestaff. The image conjured by his wife's fevered fantasy had him sweating in the darkened cabin.

"I don't think that's a good idea just yet, Christine," he said hoarsely. She sighed and closed her eyes again. She settled, her body stretched next to him. He could feel her fevered heat through his clothing.

They said at Almack's the waltz was a suggestive dance, but he'd never taken that caveat seriously until this moment. He sternly told himself only the worst kind of cad would want to remove his wife's nightclothes and fondle her lush, hot body while she raged with fever.

This time Justin sighed. It was going to be a long night.

Her fever broke just before dawn when she soaked her bedding and nightclothes with sweat. Justin ignored her protests and briskly stripped her, pulling a fresh shirt over her head and helping her to sit in a chair, wrapped in a quilt. He found fresh linens in the trunk and re-made the bunk, then carried his wife back to it and tucked her in.

She eyed her husband warily. A man who spent the night with his sick wife and performed common household tasks didn't fit with her image of the arrogant sod she'd married. He looked like hell. Hair mussed, face shadowed by beard and exhaustion. She couldn't imagine why she wanted to invite him to crawl in beside her.

"Did you really spend the night in my cabin?"

"Don't you remember?"

She frowned. A nagging headache throbbed between her eyes, but it was nothing compared to what she remembered experiencing after supper. Beyond that, though, the evening was a blank.

"Di-did something happen last night? Between us?"

Justin straightened and smiled slowly, green eyes glittering in the morning light.

"Sweetheart, you don't remember? I'm crushed, truly."

He came and sat beside her on the bunk, taking her hand in his.

"Last night," he mused. "Last night was unique. The moans. The small cries. You thrashing about. Sighing. I have never spent another night like it. Unless it was the night I held the basin while Suzanne cast up bad oysters she'd eaten."

"Idiot," she muttered, taking a weak swipe at him with her free hand. He ducked easily and laughed.

"Now, Captain Daniels, you stay in your cabin today like a good little pirate. I told Davies I'd bring you something from the galley later. Dr. Brown says only liquids for now. I will be by later to check on you. Get some rest."

Justin leaned forward and kissed her lightly on the forehead, an act that startled her into complete silence. He left the cabin, humming.

Chapter 13

Chris allowed Dr. Brown to confine her to her cabin for one full day and night, but she had work to do and a ship to run, and it didn't look good for the crew to see the captain allowing a small flesh wound to lay him out. Justin spent the day with her, bringing meals from the galley, playing cards, reading while she rested. They talked, about their childhoods and families, not about business—either the business of piracy or the business of legitimate shipping. At one point she woke and found him stretched out in a chair, his feet on the bunk, head lolling to the side. She spent long moments just watching him sleep. During the following day he was helpful and friendly with the crew, at night he was an ideal dinner companion, and not once had he tried to take advantage of her illness and steal kisses from her.

She was thoroughly irritated.

Smithton wasn't acting like he was supposed to. Where was the obnoxious Englishman who'd made fun of her in St. Augustine? Having him hovering, taking up too much space, filling the air with his spicy scent wasn't helping her stay focused on her goal. Now he was lounging on her bunk, legs stretched to the far end. His boots were off and she could see his bare feet, long and sinewy. Looking very naked.

Christine shifted uneasily in her chair. She looked down again, realized she'd been staring at the same log page for over half an hour, and cursed.

Justin watched her from beneath lowered lids. Every so often she'd pause and mutter to herself or massage her healing arm. He blew out a breath, and placed Captain Preble's *Internal Rules and Regulations* beside him on the bunk. He wasn't sure what it was doing on the *Tigress*—perhaps pirates kept the law book around for amusement. He yawned hugely. The rocking of the *Tigress* at sea and the creak of the rigging was soporific, and it was getting too easy to not think about the future.

Time to stir things up.

Justin stood, wholly aware his wife could see him at the edge of her vision. He strolled to the small railed bookshelf and ran his finger over the leather bindings.

"Do you like poetry?" He paused at a collection while the small movements at the table ceased. He looked over his shoulder as Christine sighed and ran a hand through her curls.

"I like poetry well enough. Why do you ask?"

"You are working so hard, I thought you'd enjoy a short respite. I never realized how much paperwork was involved in being a pirate captain!"

"Turning booty into dollars does not happen by magic, Smithton. If you'd been transporting specie on your ships, I might not have to work so hard."

"I apologize, Captain. Transporting specie is high risk cargo, and not for the likes of small merchants such as myself."

She snorted at this deprecating description of his profitable shipping line, but he continued.

"I have been told I have a passable reading voice," he added. "Why don't I read for a while and, if you don't like it, I will stop?"

He stood near the porthole and opened the small brown volume.

"Let us roll all our strength and all
Our sweetness up into one ball,
And tear our pleasures with rough strife
Through the iron gates of life:
Thus, though we cannot make our sun
Stand still, yet we will make him run."

Christine leaned back in her chair, eyes closed in pleasure as his deep voice lapped over her like waves of rich cream. It had been a long time since anyone had read poetry to her, and no one read her Marvell. She opened her eyes when his melodious words stopped. Justin had placed the book on the bunk and was unfastening his shirt.

Her bare feet hit the deck hard.

"What are you doing?"

He paused, his hand at the bottom stud, his open shirt showing an expanse of lightly furred chest.

"Oh, I'm sorry if I disturbed you. It was so close and warm in here, I didn't think you would mind if I got comfortable. After all," he said lightly, "I know you have seen your crew in all states of undress, you being one of the 'men' and all."

"No, of course." She cleared her throat and waved her hand. "Whatever you prefer."

"Thank you," he said, a shade too politely. Chris slouched in her chair again, her tongue darting out to lick dry lips, eyes half closed as she watched him with what she hoped was every appearance of studied disinterest.

Justin stretched his arms above his head, reaching to touch the deck above, his long legs lovingly outlined by doeskin breeches. Chris wasn't even aware she was staring at his thighs, watching the play of muscles shifting as he settled back and reached for the book.

"Oh, here's a nice one."

I'll say. Chris closed her eyes to temptation as he read on:

"What wond'rous life is this I lead!
Ripe apples drop about my head;
The luscious clusters of the vine
Upon my mouth do crush their wine;
The nectarine and curious peach,
Into my hands themselves do reach;
Stumbling on melons, as I pass,
Insnar'd with flow'rs, I fall on grass."

The last was said softly, close to her ear. Christine opened her eyes, her husband's face inches from her own as he slowly leaned forward, closing the space between them. He braced his arms on the chair, but she didn't feel trapped, and then he was kissing her, a slow, gradual process, unhurried. His lips were soft as new grass, warm as summer fruit. A strange lassitude swept through her as she leaned into his kiss, her limbs like molasses pooling in the sun. His tongue eased out to trace the line of her mouth and she gasped in surprise at the sensation. He took advantage of her vulnerability. Cupping her head, he angled his own slightly and eased his tongue into the front of her mouth until she allowed him full access. She placed her hands around his shoulders to steady herself.

When she'd dreamed of kisses while lazing in the library loft, she'd never imagined this melting awareness coursing through her veins. He was barely touching her, but she could feel his presence in every part of her body, her lips a link to his heat. He shifted his weight and stood, pulling her with him without breaking their kiss. He moved his mouth along her jawline, taking his time, gentling her and continuing the soft kisses while his hand moved lower until it curved over her rounded backside. He squeezed and was rewarded with a soft gasp that trailed to a moan under his caresses.

"I don't think..."

"Do not think, Christine, *feel*..."

She leaned into his embrace, spreading her legs for balance. He slipped his leg between hers, bracing his foot against her chair and levering his thigh high against the soft flesh outlined by her breeches. She clutched tightly at his shoulders as he brought his mouth back to hers, deepening the kiss while gently rocking his leg, allowing her time to learn how passion is built and how it grows when it is not forced or rushed.

Christine's sensations became too intense to be borne and she broke away with a small cry. Her lungs weren't pulling enough air and her legs felt limp. Had she not been clutching her husband, she'd have collapsed to the deck in a puddle. It was hard to breathe and even harder to think while he was murmuring in her ear, telling her how soft she was, how warm. Merciful heavens, no wonder the crew always seemed to be talking about intimate relations, if it aroused feelings like this! She knew she should tell him to stop, but as she rocked against his leg, all thoughts centered on the hot pressure building at her core.

He shifted suddenly and picked her up, careful of her injured arm. He carried her the few steps to her bunk and set her down on it, sitting alongside her.

"Open your eyes, Christine."

Her eyes fluttered open. He blocked the light and loomed over her, his face hard and intent. His hands stroked up and down her ribs over the thin silk of her shirt, almost as if he couldn't keep from touching her.

"Do you want this?"

His hands moved to brush his thumbs across her unbound breasts. She gasped at the sensation, arching her back to bring him even closer. She licked her lips and tried to regain control.

"This isn't wise. We should st—oh!"

His fingertips plucked at her nipples through the silk, pulling as they became engorged and hard with desire. She managed to raise her heavy eyelids to see her husband's face, sheened with sweat, his eyes glittering as he watched her body respond to his long fingers.

"Justin! This isn't a good idea!"

He grinned, a small, strained smile.

"My dear, there are parts of my body that believe this is the best idea I've ever had."

He took her hand and placed it on the hard ridge at the front of his breeches. She felt him swell beneath her grasp and then it was his turn to moan as she gently squeezed. Her objections were lost as she ran her fingers over his pulsing shaft, still trapped in his clothing yet responding to her untutored stroking. He rocked back and forth into her hand for as long as he could stand it, then forced himself to pull away. Sitting beside her on the bunk, he unfastened her shirt, but she pulled it back together and turned her head to the side, remembering another time, a different bed.

"Don't," he said in a low voice. "You should not hide your beauty."

"I'm not," she whispered. He knew without further words what she meant.

"Not beautiful? But you are, Christine. Not in the common way, but beautiful like a sword is beautiful. Beautiful like the *Tigress*, with its sleek lines."

He moved her hands and pushed her shirt aside, parting the cloth like a precious gift being unwrapped, and he gazed at her in silence, and she lay there, dreading what he would say, that even after all Christopher Daniels had accomplished, Justin would somehow still find Christine Sanders inadequate.

But he said nothing at first, only leaning down to place a soft kiss at the base of her throat, and then he spoke.

"You were beautiful before—I wasn't able to see it, though it was there." Justin's thumbs brushed back and forth across her aching nipples and she nearly wept as her passion was brought to even sharper focus.

"Beautiful then," he repeated, "and beautiful now, here. There's no ship, no loot, no running away. Just us, Christine, alone in this cabin."

He leaned down and licked one rosy nipple before cupping the mound in his hand and opening his mouth wide over her. Her low cry spurred him on, moving now to the other side to give it his attention. There was a tugging inside her, a silken cord from her breasts to her womb, intensifying and fanning the heat. She shifted her hips, her hands fisted in his raven hair, holding him closer yet.

"Oh, please," she sighed, not sure what she asked for. He stopped caressing her with his mouth and raised his head slightly.

"Oh yes, sweetheart, I'm going to please you," he said, licking the underside of her breast for emphasis. "We'll always be good together, you'll see."

His words sent a small warning into her brain, but whatever the warning, it was forgotten as he reared back on his knees to flick open the buttons of her breeches while she watched. The wide-legged trousers slid easily down her legs and off the bunk, then the backs of his fingers brushed the inside of her thighs and made her shiver. As he moved back from her into the light and took off his clothes, she watched. She knew she could stop this with a word, but she needed to know what it was she kept reaching for in her dreams. She needed to exorcise her demons, and the fire raging in her blood offered answers.

But she didn't know if they were the right answers.

His shirt joined her trousers on the deck, then he sat on the edge of the bunk to undo his breeches. She couldn't resist touching him as he sat there, absorbing the heat from his body as she ran her hand along his back and his ribs, and he went still, tension evident in every harsh line as she learned his body. When she leaned into him, her breasts pressing into his back and her hands brushing the planes of his belly, it was his turn to gasp and close his eyes. Her fingers moved to his chest and she used her fingertips to pluck his nipples as he had hers. So similar and so different, the solid muscles moving beneath his skin, his light curls that rasped against her fingers.

"Bloody hell," he gritted, eyes closed, head thrown back. She licked the side of his neck while he fumbled open the fastenings on his trousers, then she glanced over his shoulder and gasped as he sprang free. It had been one thing to see her husband when he was naked and relaxed. Aroused, he was more than she'd expected, much more than she remembered. He turned his head and captured her lips with his while his hand firmly grasped hers and moved it from his chest to his groin. He wrapped her hand around his shaft and moaned into her mouth when she began stroking, lightly at first, then firmer as he thrust into her fist.

Justin broke the kiss and levered her back down, covering her body with his. Pushing his trousers and small clothes off with one hand, he used his other to stroke through the damp curls between her thighs. She was wet and swollen and he eased a finger into her opening. She was so tight he almost hesitated, but then she whimpered and raised her hips, seeking more. He settled in the cradle of her thighs, arms alongside hers and brushed the curls out of her eyes.

"Almost there, love. Just a moment longer."

Justin was more affected by his wife's untutored passion than he'd expected. Her long frame fit in his arms as if she were made for him and he felt with this woman, he didn't have to hold back. She was strong and sized to suit him, her body pliant, her tensile strength and supple curves balanced by her grace. But there was still much about her that was fragile as a crystal drop, ready to shatter at a clumsy touch.

He set his mouth on hers lightly as he probed between her legs. Sliding into her on an indrawn breath, he swallowed her gasp with his mouth and rested there a moment, allowing her time to adjust before he brushed his hands down her sides to her hips, grasping her firmly and tilting her toward him. He almost exploded into her then, but knew he had to make it perfect for her.

"Wrap your legs around me...Yes, like that." He began moving, establishing a rhythm she quickly caught.

Christine looked up into the shadows. His eyes were closed, his head thrown back, a look of intense concentration distorting his features. For a moment, she flashed back to that disastrous wedding night, then the feelings rolled over her in a wave and she arched her back, wanting more.

This was different from before, but no less terrifying. She couldn't control the sensations flaming along her skin, the longing deep inside her. The heat between her thighs was growing and she was racing, racing toward a goal that was just out of reach. His movements speeded up and he was rocking into her with long, powerful strokes. Her hands clenched and unclenched on his back as she kept reaching. Then he slipped his hand between their bodies, touching a small, swollen button and suddenly she was *there*, a strangled cry coming from deep within her soul.

Everything exploded from that hot core and, as her arms clamped around him, her inner muscles clenched, driving him over his own edge to a shattering conclusion. There was one final thrust, then warmth, and he relaxed on top of her, panting as she did. There wasn't enough air in the cabin for both of them.

Justin rolled to the side, still inside her, not releasing his grip on his wife. Christine fell asleep in his arms, rocked by the gentle motion of the *Tigress*.

"Nothing's changed!"

"Bloody hell, nothing's changed! Everything has changed!"

Justin scowled at his wife as she sat on the side of the bunk, yanking on her boots. How the hell had they reached this point? One moment, they were sharing the most explosive lovemaking he'd ever experienced, finally feeling some absolution for that fiasco of a wedding night, and now they were back at dagger's point. He glared as she reached inside her striped pantaloons to adjust her codpiece, and then she stood.

"It is time for you to return to your cabin, Justin." Her eyes slid away from his. "Tomorrow we will be putting in for fresh water at a river. It is about a day's journey from Savannah for a man on foot."

He went still.

"You will abandon me there?"

"As I told you, we'll leave you with provisions, maps, and your weapons, and a pack with your personal belongings. Your trunks will be sent to St. Augustine. By the time you make it to the city, we'll be gone."

He stared at her, not believing what he was hearing. Her face was shuttered, her stance wide-legged and straight. Whoever had shared the bunk with him so sweetly was gone, replaced by Captain Daniels.

"I don't understand. I thought we had come to know one another well. I thought you cared for me. What is so terrible about being my wife?"

"We already had this conversation, Justin! You tell me what has changed! We have gotten to know one another better, we have become lovers, yes. But it is not enough. Not for me. Don't you see? In England, you will go back to your life, your businesses—what would I do? Do not be fooled by this interlude." Christine waved her hand around the cabin. "This is make-believe. I know that. Soon it will end and our real lives resume."

He ran his hand through his hair in exasperation and began to pace the cabin. "Other women of our class don't seem unsatisfied. They have entertainments and shopping, visiting neighbors and tenants at the estates and… I...I don't know, you could involve yourself in charitable works. We'll raise a family," he finished softly, stopping before her.

He lifted his hand as if to touch her hair, but left it hovering in the air. She shook her head, looking down at the deck.

"It won't work, Justin. I am not of your class. I am a merchant's daughter. All my life, I have been raised to run Sanders. I expected to marry a local merchant, not an English earl. I know schedules and debit sheets and trade. I would not fit in with the ton and I would be an embarrassment to you and your family."

She sniffed and raised her head, giving him a watery smile. "Mayhap I'd revert to my old ways and take up smuggling in Devonshire. Just think how that would go over with your fine friends."

Justin could hear a pounding in his ears like the tide rushing out and he moved, grabbing her and pulling her against him.

"And this? This means nothing?"

He brought his mouth down on hers, hard. One hand shifted around her waist while the other buried itself in her hair, holding her captive.

His mouth ravaged hers, a punishing kiss, and she made a small mewl of discomfort. Instantly, his mouth gentled until he broke away, holding her tight against him.

"And what of this, Christine?" he whispered against her cheek. "Do you not need this as well? You are so beautifully responsive—who will stroke you and rouse you when I'm gone?"

She shuddered against him, but she pulled away.

"It is not enough, Justin."

"It is more than most have! Far more than I ever hoped for from this marriage!"

"Yes, well, it may be more than you expected, but if you recall I did not want to be married to you at all! Did it not occur to you that I have higher expectations? The expectation that I would find a man who wanted me for what I was, who loved me?"

Something flashed through him, an anger he couldn't name. "Is there someone else?"

"On this ship? Not bloody likely! No, there is no one else, Justin. That is not the issue!" Now it was her turn to glare at him.

"You have never understood what I wanted and I am not going to settle for your idea of what a proper marriage is! Your dreams are not *my* dreams. I want more than that. I want to be more than some lordling's latest acquisition. I want my own life! And I will have it, now that have the means to live independently!"

Her words fell over him like a firestorm, but it was ice that he felt, ice that froze his face into an impassive mask as he stepped away from her.

"This is not over," he said in a low voice. "I will leave you for now, madam, to your money and your trade and your independence. And I trust that, in the absence of a husband, they will bring you comfort on a winter's night."

He bowed slightly, turned his back and left the cabin, the hand that had caressed her clenched at his side.

Christine stared at the closed hatch. She wanted to scream. She wanted to throw something. She wanted to cry.

Captains don't do those things, not in close quarters. She took a deep breath, and looked in the mirror. And for a moment gave herself the indulgence of hating the young man who stared back. Then she splashed water on her face, dried it, and calmly darkened her upper lip. She adjusted her hat to shade her eyes and went up on deck.

Julius was at the wheel. He looked at her face and sighed.

"You told Smithton about tomorrow."

"I told Smithton about tomorrow. He did not take the news well."

She looked at the coast, barely seen in the distance. "Congratulate me, Jules," she said huskily. "I have gotten everything I wanted and worked for. Am I not the most fortunate of souls?"

That night she stayed in her cabin, pleading fatigue from her illness. When Robin brought her supper tray, the young man said the earl was also not coming to supper. A hopeless romantic, he sighed deeply as he set down her dinner.

Two hours later, the tray still sat untouched on the table. Christine was rolling a mug of rum between her hands, staring into a slightly swaying lantern, when a knock came at her cabin. Thinking it was Robin, she opened the hatch.

Her husband looked down at her, his eyes shadowed in the dark corridor.

"We said our good-byes, Justin."

"We said a lot of things today, Christine." He reached out and this time did touch her hair, lightly, caressing the curl looped behind her ear. "Must we spend our last night bitter with one another? I already have some wonderful memories to take with me. Let us create a few more, together."

"Come," she said finally, inviting him in. He stooped, stopped, and sniffed close to her as he passed, frowning as he entered the cabin. It was aglow in the lantern light and the small sounds of a ship at night drifted in the porthole. Chris closed the hatch and leaned against it. She could see him studying her, the disordered hair, the slight swaying that had nothing to do with the roll of the ship.

"You are drunk."

"No, but I was making good progress when you knocked. I am sober enough to know I shouldn't have let you in. And I'm drunk enough to want you to stay." In a low voice she said, "Take off your clothes."

He stared at her.

"What?"

"I'm creating memories. You chose to come, you pay the forfeit. Start with your shirt."

He silently looked at her a moment longer, then began on his cuffs, his eyes never leaving hers. He shrugged the shirt off and waited as it slid down his body to the deck. He wore nothing beneath, and she sucked in a deep breath.

"Now the boots."

"I'll need help."

She gestured to the bunk and he sat, waiting. She cocked her head to one side, looking a bit longer at the hard muscles of his bare chest, then walked slowly and carefully across to the bunk. She knelt in front of his legs and pulled off his right boot, then his left, rocking back on her heels with the effort. Then putting a hand on each buckskin-clad knee, she eased his legs apart and scooted forward.

His breath caught as he looked at her kneeling at his feet, and Christine imagined in this position she looked deceptively vulnerable. She would have to do something about that. Turning her head, she kissed his inner thigh. He gripped the edge of the bunk and she leaned back on her heels. That was showing him. When one captained a ship called *Tigress,* one had certain standards to uphold.

"Now unbutton your breeches."

Christine looked up into his eyes and saw he wasn't as passive as he appeared. The pulse at the base of his neck throbbed and she resisted the impulse to reach up and lick it. It was a pleasure she'd save for later. Like her ship's namesake, she'd toy with her prey before moving in for the kill. Never breaking her gaze, his hand reached down and undid the fastenings.

"Now take your cock out." She smiled at his body's reaction, pleased her very words could arouse him.

"I'll need help," he repeated hoarsely. She smiled again and, taking his hands in hers, placed them on the edge of the bunk alongside his thighs.

"Don't move," she breathed, leaning forward. She wrapped one hand around the calf of his leg, feeling muscles twitch, and with the other hand ran her knuckles along the bulge before her, once, twice, each time rewarded with a convulsive response. His hands turned white at the joints as he gripped the bunk per her orders. It was good he was obeying. The night was far from over. She eased inside the opening, reaching through to free him, and he overflowed her hand as she stroked him. Justin's head was thrown back, the cords on his neck standing out in sharp relief.

"Dear God, don't stop!"

"Stop?" she murmured, "Not till you cry 'quarter.' A true pirate shows no mercy."

She leaned forward and licked him, running her tongue along his length from the base to the very tip. He swore again, a strangled sound.

It didn't sound like 'quarter,' so she repeated her action. Then she took him inside her mouth, cradling his hot sack in her hand with a slight rolling motion. He was definitely making sounds of distress now, but his hands were still tight on the bunk.

She admired his discipline, even as she moved her head back a tad to run her tongue along the small slit at his tip.

That broke him. His hands fisted in her hair, drawing her closer. She allowed this breach of discipline for a few moments, then pulled back while pushing him flat against the bedding.

"Stay still, Smithton, or I'll have to tie you to the bunk."

A hot grin slashed across his face and he raised his arms over his head, tucking his hands beneath her pillow. The muscles in his arms stood out like hawsers.

"I am your prisoner, Captain Daniels. I cannot stop you from having your wicked way with me."

"Now that's what we pirates like! A bit of cooperation during the ol' slap and tickle." She sat astride him, pulling off his remaining clothes, then rocked back on her heels, taking a long, leisurely look at her prisoner.

"You really do look good naked, Justin, and believe me, I have seen my share of unclothed men 'round here."

He scowled, but she soothed his expression with a kiss, her lips lingering against his. He arched his back, seeking contact with her body, but she pulled away with a small, catlike smile at his groan of frustration. He kept his hands locked beneath the pillow. Well disciplined, indeed.

She shimmied off the bunk and unbuttoned her own clothes. Not as slowly as Justin, but he watched intently nonetheless. Unwrapping her breasts with a quickness born of practice, Christine smiled at his indrawn breath when she was undone and open to his gaze.

Returning to the bunk, she eased over him so they were face to face, limb to limb. She lowered her hips until he was poised at her entrance, then slowly rubbed herself against his length. She was enjoying every moment of control, the feel of him sliding back and forth between her legs, hitting every sensitive spot in her swollen, slick folds. She enjoyed the illusion of having him at her command, the way he gave without seizing his own satisfaction. Finally, she decided to have mercy on her captive and slowly, very slowly, eased down until, inch by inch, he slid into her. She drew her breath in with a hiss and when she'd taken him into the root, she leaned forward, her eyes two glowing slits in the dim light. Moving his hands from beneath the pillow, she held them fast alongside his head. Gazing into his eyes, she began moving, a gentle rocking motion at first, then picking up speed as she found her rhythm, and his.

Passion spiraled upward, drawing her higher and higher. She released his hands and he seized her, pulling her down so he could plunge his tongue inside her mouth, stealing her breath as she climaxed. She tore her mouth from his and muffled her cry in the pillow as he in turn peaked, his back arching like a bow as he clutched her, her contractions milking his own release.

"Quarter!" he gasped, and fell back on the bunk.

Her lips curled in a wan smile as a lone tear leaked from the corner of her eye. She wiped it on the pillow before he could notice.

"Too late."

The summer morning was bright and promised later heat as the *Tigress* rocked at anchor in a cove off the Georgia coast. A landing crew made ready to fetch fresh water. Along with the casks were the personal possessions of Justin Delerue, Earl Smithton.

Justin came abovedecks looking self-possessed and calm. Only Christine, who'd spent the night in his arms, knew it was a pose. She joined him at the rail, away from the others.

"You will not change your mind."

It was a statement, not a question.

"No. My course is set, Justin. After today, we go our separate ways. When you have documents for me, post word in the *Gazette* and then we'll be finished," she said in a low voice.

He gently took her shoulder and turned her so she was facing him, not the coast. "Do you really believe that, Chris?"

"Yes." She looked into eyes reflecting the lush green of the vegetation on shore. Last night, they'd darkened to nearly black as, over and over again, he'd created memories with her. She reached up and brushed an errant curl back from his forehead. "It won't work, Justin. There isn't enough there, not nearly enough."

He looked at her steadily and shook his head. "It's not over yet, Christine. We still have unfinished business. And I don't mean a divorce. What if you find yourself increasing?"

Her hand jerked to her abdomen. She'd been incredibly foolish not to think of that first. For an instant, an image flashed through her mind of a black-haired, emerald-eyed little boy smiling up at her, but she shook her head.

"It is unlikely after one night together." She raised her hand to forestall him as he started to speak. "It is a possibility. I'll know soon enough, time to get word to you before you leave St. Augustine. If I find that I am with child, I will come with you."

He cocked his head to the side and studied her wan face. "You could wait it out and give me the babe."

Her hand went to the dagger at her hip and she stepped back.

"Give up my child? Not for all the riches in England, Smithton!"

He startled her by smiling broadly.

"I am pleased there are things money can't buy, Captain Daniels. Now, don't get your dander up. As you say, it is a slim possibility. Care to go below and try again?"

"How can you joke at a time like this?"

He stepped forward so they were only a handsbreadth apart and placed his long fingers beneath her chin, tilting her face up to his.

"The difference, my dear Captain, is that you think this is good-bye and I don't."

He leaned forward, then halted, color high on his cheeks. For a moment, he'd forgotten on the *Tigress* he would be kissing Captain *Christopher* Daniels. It was Christine's turn to smile at her husband's discomfort, and she stepped back a pace to give him a moment to compose himself.

"Listen to me, Justin. I still want that divorce, but with or without it, I will go ahead with my life. I am not going to let a piece of paper stop me now."

He quirked one arrogant eyebrow. "Let us take it one day at a time for now, shall we? Who knows, Captain, perhaps you too, will suffer a sea change before we are done."

He went quietly with the landing crew, and Christine watched him watching her from shore until he was out of sight, and out of her life.

Chapter 14

Six months later

It was a busy evening at the riverside tavern called Ganymede's Cup, a tavern with a reputation up and down the coast. Simpkins had taken a generous offer for the tavern, as usual, not caring where the gold came from as long as it was good. The refurbished establishment was attracting trade from all over, lured by stories of delectable meals, clean beds, and discreet owners.

Justin was counting on that discretion as he and Peter Marlowe finished an outstanding supper of corn chowder, turkey with rice and oyster dressing, sweet potato pie, venison steaks, and fine wines. Peter leaned back in satisfaction.

"That may be the best meal I have had since I arrived in Florida. How did you know about this tavern?"

"I have my sources," Justin said, his eyes scanning the crowded public room. He sat near the kitchen with a clear view of the front entrance. Cooper was behind the bar and had only raised an eyebrow when the earl strolled in. He did, however, take a club out from underneath and lay it on the bar, close to hand.

"Tell me about this person we are meeting tonight. Is it really that pirate captain who held you prisoner? I don't understand why you don't alert the authorities and have him clapped in chains." Peter shook his head. "It is not like you to allow someone to wrong you and walk away. And what about the money and the cargo?"

"Peter, Peter, you see everything as black-and-white issues," Justin said, his lips curling. "Sometimes when you spend time with a fellow, things are revealed that give you an entirely new perspective. We have not had a ship robbed since I met with Captain Daniels, correct?"

He flashed Peter a smile. "After all, I am told, in all modesty, that I have a charming and winning manner. I am confident I persuaded the captain to find other targets for his piratical forays and so our ships remain safe, at least from the notorious Christopher Daniels."

"I don't think I want to hear more about it," Peter muttered, glancing nervously at The Greek Boy's patrons. "I have heard rumors of exactly what Captain Christopher Daniels is notorious *for*."

Justin looked at his friend, all humor gone. "I need you to be calm and clearheaded tonight, Peter. There may be trouble before the evening is gone, but if you follow my lead, all will be well."

"Whatever you need, Justin, I'm your man." Peter said stoutly.

Shortly before eight, Peter glanced up to see a tall man in a stylish coat of blue satin with red buttons the size of saucers standing in the doorway. Cooper nodded to him and cocked his head toward Justin's table. Peter shifted in his seat as Captain Daniels stared at them for the longest time. Justin just watched his nemesis, calm as ever.

Daniels raised a hand in salute to Cooper and walked across the room with a light mincing step, not stopping to answer the greetings from the tavern's regulars, eyes glued to the two Englishmen in the corner. The pirate sat across from Justin and Peter, huge chocolate eyes unblinking, waiting for the conversation to open.

"Peter," Justin drawled, "It is unconscionably rude of you not to greet my wife."

Peter's eyes grew nearly as large as the buttons on Christine's coat as he stared at her.

"Christine? Lady Smithton?" He goggled and whipped his head 'round to gape at Justin. "You married a *man*?"

Christine choked and coughed to hide her laughter.

Justin sighed.

"Don't be an idiot, Peter. Christine has been disguising her sex and hiding from me these past months."

"But...but...this is the pirate who robbed us!"

"Yes, well, one has to keep busy," Christine said in a low voice. "Hello, Peter. Justin."

"I don't understand any of t—wait, that is how you knew my name aboard the *Phoenix*!"

Christine tore her eyes away from her husband's face and smiled at his friend. "I am sorry about ruffling your feathers that day, Peter. I trust you and Lady Suzanne were able to settle safely in St. Augustine?"

"Suzanne?" Peter said, still staring. "Oh, yes, Suzanne! We were married two months ago. She's fine. You have a moustache!"

This time Christine didn't try to suppress her husky laughter. Justin blew his breath out and looked up at the ceiling as if seeking divine guidance.

"Peter," he said. "Go sit by the bar."

"By myself!?" Peter squeaked.

Christine grinned hugely. "Don't worry, Peter. Cooper won't let anyone bother you. Please give Justin and me some privacy. He went to a lot of trouble to arrange this meeting, and I would like to hear what he has to say. Oh, and best wishes to you on your wedding."

Peter hurried to the bar and leaned against it, nursing a glass of whisky while keeping a wary eye on the tavern. He was passed by Robin, bustling out from the kitchen and wiping his hands on his apron, beaming at the couple seated across from each other at the table.

"Smithton! And Cap'n Daniels! I knew it, I just knew it. I kept telling Richard over and over you two were meant to be together and here you are! Oh, I'm so happy I could just burst!"

"It lacked only this," Justin murmured.

"Hello, Robin," Chris said with a warm smile for her former cook. "How goes the tavern business?"

"Oh, Cap'n, it's so good to have you here again!" Robin turned to Justin and lowered his voice conspiratorially. "The Cap'n's been pining, absolutely pining, since we put you ashore. Hardly eats enough to keep a rabbit alive."

"Really?" Justin glanced at his wife with keen interest. She was scowling now and bright red flagged her cheekbones. It was his turn to smile. "You never know how things will turn out, do you, Robin? Why don't you bring the Captain a cup of coffee and a slice of that excellent rum cake I enjoyed earlier, and I will see if I can pique his appetite."

He leaned back in his chair with a self-satisfied smirk Chris longed to slap from his face. But she was afraid that if she touched that sun-bronzed skin, she'd end up caressing it. He was just as she remembered through the lonely nights, his eyes as glowing green, his sculpted lips looking as kissable as they had aboard the *Tigress.*

"What did you think when you saw the notice in the *Gazette*, Chris?"

"'Gentleman has business proposition to discuss with Captain C. Daniels?'" She shrugged, pulling off her gloves. "I thought it might be you, though it could have been any number of people. After all, I have got numerous investments demanding my attention. However, I also figured if it was you, it must be important to bring you here in hurricane season."

"I believe this trip is important and we have much to discuss. That reminds me. Where is that oversized protector of yours?"

"He will drop by later," she lied. Julius was in Cowford buying supplies, but she didn't think Smithton needed that information.

They paused while Robin set down a large mug of coffee and a slice of nut-filled cake so steeped in rum the aroma wafted clear off the table.

"Smithton, you wouldn't be trying to befuddle my senses with this cake, would you?" Christine looked askance at the decadent dessert.

"Me?" He was all innocence. "How could I ever pull one over the fierce master of the *Tigress*?"

Robin leaned in close to the earl. "Julius says Cap'n Daniel's been tough to live with. Megrims and nervous energy, if you get my drift. Maybe you can do something."

Christine put her fork down, carefully, on the table and took a deep breath.

"Go away, Robin. Now. Stop laughing, Smithton, or I'll shoot you myself."

Little laugh lines fanned out from Justin's eyes, and he struggled manfully to get himself under control. She did look angry enough to shoot him, but he was enjoying sitting across from her, feeling her energy and warmth again. She was thinner than when he'd left her, and still looked captivating for all that. Even with a mustache penciled on her lips.

"Robin," Chris said sternly, "go back to your galley."

"Thank you, Robin. Is Cooper trying to catch your eye?" Justin nodded toward the bar.

"Who's that toff with him?" Robin frowned, pulling at his lower lip.

"Relax, Robin, that is my brother-in-law, Peter Marlowe. Remember him from the *Phoenix*?"

"Of course! He was very protective of the young lady, your sister. And now they're married! How delightful!" He hurried over to offer his congratulations to Peter and chat with Richard, a maneuver allowing him to keep an eye on Captain Daniels's table. Richard was absolutely useless at passing along important information.

"Now, Chris, don't poker up at me. I did come here to talk. And eat Robin's cooking again." He switched, like a ship tacking in the wind. "Are you enjoying your freedom?"

"Yes!" she snapped. "I have been making money hand over fist and have long-term investments that will provide income for years to come. I am supremely content." She stabbed the rum cake.

"Are you planning on spending the rest of your life as Christopher Daniels?"

"No. Christopher Daniels will have an unfortunate and fatal accident in the near future, witnessed by Julius and Dr. Brown, who, you might wish to know, is a highly respected member of St. Augustine society. Don't go trying to stir up trouble for Brown. Believe me, his reputation will withstand the scrutiny."

Justin raised his eyebrows at this. Christine had thought ahead to a life without him, and must be confident of his intentions if she revealed so much. He told Peter he was known for being charming and winning.

It better be true tonight.

Christine pushed away the rest of her cake, took a deep swallow of the hot coffee and leaned forward, arms crossed on the table. As she moved toward him he caught the scent that was uniquely hers, sandalwood and jasmine, and all he wanted to do was to bury his hands in those gold-brushed curls and kiss her senseless.

"I'm here. Talk."

Justin sighed. It had been a nice fantasy.

"So much for social pleasantries." He looked at her intently and lowered his voice. "I have been busy these past six months, shoring up Delerue-Sanders Shipping after its disasters at the hands of your crew. Don't glare, it *is* Delerue-Sanders, and all the wishing and piracy in Florida isn't going to get it back in your hands. Florida law reflects English law, for the most part. You cannot own the company all by yourself, Christine, not while you are married to me.

"I will not give you a divorce, Christine."

She didn't leap up from the table, curse him or stab him and storm out. He released his breath. She was sitting very, very still, like a cornered animal waiting to see what its attacker's next move was.

She finally spoke, expressionlessly. "Is there more?"

"Yes." He took a drink of his brandy, watched her drink her coffee, then continued. "I have made new arrangements and rewritten my will. The first change is that, if I die, you, Christine Sanders Delerue, inherit a portion of Delerue-Sanders shipping as well as a widow's jointure from my estate and the usual endowments. Peter and Suzanne have decided to stay in St. Augustine. He had limited prospects as a younger son in England, and actually likes this beastly climate. Peter will run Delerue-Sanders's Florida operation for me and own a minority share. The shipping company will operate better with someone I trust at the helm.

"I am returning to England on the *Griffin*. Soon."

She stirred at this last comment, but said nothing.

He lowered his voice to a near whisper that held her attention more firmly than a shout.

"It is the best I can do, my dear Captain. I cannot give you the shipping company while I am alive, only my death would give you complete freedom. I hope you will see this as good faith on my part."

He stared at her a moment longer, then ran his hand through his hair, disarranging the black locks. He looked down at his brandy and sighed.

"The ton isn't known for producing good marriages, Christine. My parents were not happy together, and I know few married couples who seem to truly enjoy each other's company. But we do."

He looked up at her, straining to read her expression. "I have watched Peter and Suzanne these past months. Yes, she's dependent on him, but he's dependent on her too. He depends on her to give him comfort and affection, to make him laugh, and to scold him when he is wrong. It is not one-sided, but a partnership of give and take." He smiled. "Come back with me to England and be my partner. Together, we will make a future for our children."

His smile grew larger. "We will be like Richard and Robin, only more conventional."

He reached across the scarred table to take her ungloved hand. She pulled it back, out of reach, looked down at the table, then brought her eyes back up to his.

"I appreciate the changes in your will, really, but I would never wish for your death so I could profit from it. As for what Robin and Richard have, there are differences." Her hand tightened 'round the mug. "Richard can't take Robin's assets, small as they are. And they have something that's more than a business partnership, or even a deep friendship.

"You've not made it clear why you want me with you rather than someone more suitable."

He shifted uneasily in his seat, glancing around the tavern. "You know how I feel!"

"No, I do not know how you feel, Justin. I know it would be easier for you this way. But you do have other options."

This time she left her hand atop the table, and her face was as open and exposed as the veins pulsing in her wrist.

"Why *me*, Justin?"

"It looks like I'll get no quarter from you tonight, Captain Daniels." He took a deep breath and clasped her hand, linking it tightly with his. He stared at their joined hands a moment, then raised his head.

"Come with me because I love you, Chris! I want you, and only you, always by my side!"

This pronouncement occurred at the same time as one of those strange conversational lulls that can occur, where even in a crowded tavern noise flows away and something said in perfectly normal tones fills a room.

Justin looked around wildly for a moment at the silent faces staring at them, then released her and dropped his head into his hands.

"Oh, Christ."

Christine looked dazed, her eyes glowing. But whatever response she was going to make was forestalled by a shriek from the bar.

"That's the most romantic thing I've ever heard!" cried Robin, and throwing his apron up over his face, burst into tears. Richard reached across the bar and awkwardly patted him on the neck.

"Oi! What are those shirtlifters goin' on about now?" snarled a grizzled drover in the corner.

"Who you callin' a shirtlifter, ya bastritch!" yelled the man at the next table.

That, and one sloppily thrown punch, was all it took to get Cooper leaping over the bar, club in hand, while pandemonium broke out along with the fisticuffs.

Christine ducked as a glass whizzed by her ear and yelled, "Behind you, Justin!" before pulling her husband down and away from a chair that would have connected with his head.

"Thank y—" he started, but finished by clawing his way up from the floor and out from underneath a porky and redolent body that had landed on top of him where he'd been pulled to safety.

By his wife. Who was now snarling and trading blows with a French sailor.

"Chris!" he yelled, a mistake, as it caused her to turn her head just in time to take a blow on the chin. It knocked her off her feet and her head connected smartly with the table behind her.

Justin roared and went after the Frenchman. No fool he, the sailor saw Death bearing down on him, and turned and ran.

"Peter! Over here!"

Peter managed to make it through the melee to Justin where he kneeled next to Christine. Justin lightly slapped her face. She looked at him groggily, then sank under again.

The opportunity was heaven sent. Justin mentally vowed to give the vicar the funds he'd been asking for to fix the parish church roof.

"I'm getting her out of here. Guard my back."

He hoisted Christine over his shoulder and, with Peter's help, kicked and pushed his way out the back door to where his men waited at the riverside.

Chapter 15

Justin entered the boat and Peter passed his wife down to him. Peter then climbed in and at Justin's direction, fished out a cloak from a valise he'd put in the boat earlier. Justin wet a handkerchief with river water and wiped off his wife's moustache, wrapped Christine in the cloak and cradled her on his lap, carefully supporting her head against his shoulder. Flashes of moonlight between tree branches illumined her face, calm in sleep. The men began rowing on the river, a lantern in the bow lighting their way. Off in the dark a hunting cat yowled and Justin held his wife closer.

"When she awakens, she's going to have your liver for luncheon."

Justin sighed. "Thank you for the reminder."

Feeling beneath the cloak, he pulled her dagger from its sheath and quickly patted her down. There was a pistol in her coat pocket, also removed for safekeeping.

"I take it you're planning on having her leave with you tonight regardless of her wishes?"

"Yes," Justin said firmly. "But it is going to work out. We just need time together."

"Who are you trying to convince, Justin, me or yourself?" Peter watched his friend cradle the woman he loved in his arms and suddenly a quiet and dull life in St. Augustine looked more attractive than ever. "I don't envy you, but if it works out it will all be for the best."

"Wish me luck, old friend. I've fought pirates and built holdings on two continents, but this is the toughest battle I've ever faced."

He smiled bleakly. "England hasn't always fared well in its dealings with America. Let us hope I can turn the tide this time in favor of Britannia."

They continued in silence until they reached the harbor. Christine stirred once or twice, but remained unconscious, her breathing even. Peter disembarked and with a firm handclasp and a whispered "Godspeed," was off for his home and the comfort of his reassuringly conventional wife's arms.

The crew rowed out to the *Griffin* where Justin carried her to his cabin, issuing terse commands to the captain of his ship, and dispatching the boat back to town one more time.

Christine woke the next morning to the roll of a ship under sail and a view of an unfamiliar deck overhead.

"Good morning. Does your head hurt?"

She slowly turned, a headache pounding between her eyes. Her husband sat in a chair next to her bunk, unshaven, wearing the same clothes he'd had on in the tavern. He looked as bad as she felt.

"Where am I?"

Without answering, he leaned forward and raised her slightly to drink from the cup of water he held. She drank thirstily, then pushed the cup back. Justin sat back in his chair and rolled the cup between his hands, looking at her from shadowed eyes.

"We're on the *Griffin*, bound for England. We have been at sea for some hours now."

She turned her head away from him, looked up at the deck overhead, and frowned.

"The last thing I remember, I'd gone to meet you at Ganymede's Cup. There was a fight, and—and you were trying to tell me something."

"You don't remember our conversation?"

She rubbed her forehead. "You were trying to convince me to come with you. I know I didn't say yes." She rolled toward him with effort. Her head felt like it might collapse inward.

"You took me from the tavern and put me on a ship for England while I was senseless?"

He jumped to his feet, pacing back and forth in the narrow cabin before slamming his hand against the hatch and glaring at her.

"Dammit, Christine, grow up! You are *not* a pirate but my countess, my chattel, and my responsibility!" He took a deep breath. "I asked you on the *Tigress* to come with me and you refused. I am done asking, Lady Smithton. Your place is at your husband's side!"

She swung her legs over the side of the bunk. Someone—she presumed her husband—had stripped off her clothes and dressed her in a night rail. She sat for a moment with her head between her hands, then looked up. He watched her warily, legs braced against the roll of the ship.

"You think you can just take what you want?"

"Why not?" he snarled. "You did!"

He stopped, scrubbing at his face for a moment. "Dear God, Christine, this isn't how I wanted it to be. Neither one of us is fit right now to hold a conversation. I will have breakfast brought to you. Stay in here today and rest. I expect you to join Captain Jackson and me for supper. Maybe—maybe you will also remember the other things I told you last night."

Without waiting for her response, he turned on his heel and left.

Christine sat on the bunk, hands clenched until they stopped shaking. It had only taken a few minutes for everything to come crashing down—all the time, effort, and blood and she was back where she started, a prisoner of her husband. Her eyes narrowed as she mentally shook herself.

She wasn't back where she'd started. The girl who ran away on her wedding night didn't exist anymore and "Captain Daniels" was as much a part of her as the other Christine Sanders had been.

And the man who'd stormed out of the cabin wasn't the same man who'd treated her so negligently in St. Augustine.

Her lips pursed as she looked around. There were two trunks in the cabin. Justin's toiletries were laid out and a smaller case revealed a set of women's hair brushes and supplies. She washed at the basin and carefully combed her short curls, wincing when she felt the back of her head, still tender from its blow in the tavern. There was no blood though.

After washing she felt better and explored the larger of the trunks, filled with women's clothing. A morning dress of soft blue muslin with a stomacher bodice and *gigot* sleeves was near the top and she tried it on, amazed at the close fit. She held out her arm, examining the sleeves. Styles had changed since the last time she'd dressed as a woman, but Smithton, or whomever had ordered the clothing, seemed to know what was *la mode* in women's fashions.

She was fastening the last of the tapes when there was a knock at the hatch. A young seaman was on the other side, balancing a tray of covered dishes.

"I've brought breakfast, yer ladyship."

"Thank you," she said, pulling up a smile. This produced a bright red flush in the sailor's cheeks and he hurried to set the tray down on the table.

"What's your name, sailor?"

"Tom, milady. Thomas Watkins. I'm the *Griffin's* cabin boy, mum."

"I have a request, young Thomas. Would you please see that these garments are laundered and returned to me?"

He took the pile of men's clothing from her and frowned. He

sometimes acted as Lord Smithton's valet at sea and knew the foppish clothes were too small for the earl. But it wasn't his place to ask, so he agreed to wash and return them the next day.

Breakfast helped restore Christine's equilibrium and took away most of the ache in her head. Afterward, she searched the cabin, but found neither her dagger nor her pistol.

On a shelf above the bunk, though, was a familiar object. Her hands brushed lightly over the leather-bound book she'd slipped into Justin's belongings when he'd left the *Tigress.* It fell open to a well-thumbed page.

It had been easy fighting in some plain,
Where victory might hang in equal choice,
But all resistance against her is vain,
Who has the advantage both of eyes and voice,
And all my forces needs must be undone,
She having gained both the wind and sun.

Her eyes misted. Unfair! Smithton was pulling out the 36-pounders and leaving her luffing in the wind against a man who made her laugh, fed her rum cake, and read her favorite poetry.

She slammed the small volume shut—issues were yet to be resolved before she melted into a puddle of uxorious bliss.

Christine rested for a while longer in the cabin before the midday heat drove her topside. A chip straw bonnet was stowed aboard and its ribbons fluttered gaily in the sea breeze as she climbed the ladder and cursed all women's dress designers for buggerin' sods. The long, narrow skirts hampered her strides across the deck and made it more difficult to find her sea legs.

Justin raised his brows as his wife navigated toward him, thinking for a moment she resembled her ship under full sail more than a countess. On the other hand, he'd seen countesses at Almack's who resembled barkentines, so perhaps the comparison wasn't so far-fetched.

"What are you grinning at?"

"Nothing, my dove. Allow me to introduce Captain Jackson."

The *Griffin's* captain had been told Christine was in Florida recovering from a lengthy illness. Captain Chandler Jackson raised a shaggy eyebrow as he watched her ladyship's energetic strides across the ship, but he valued his job and wasn't about to question the state of affairs between the ship's owner and his wife. He chatted briefly with Lady Smithton about the weather, then excused himself, leaving the couple alone at the starboard rail.

"It's good to see you up and about, Christine. That dress looks lovely on you. However, you are missing an ornament."

He reached into his waistcoat pocket and pulled out a box with two rings. One was the wedding band she'd removed the night she'd fled. The other was a betrothal ring, a sapphire of midnight blue surrounded by diamonds. Justin carefully removed her gloves and slipped on the rings, the wedding band sliding easily onto its proper finger. He stared at them a moment before gazing into her eyes and raising her hands to his lips for a kiss.

"Now they are where they belong."

She said nothing as he tucked her arm inside his and began strolling the deck.

"Are you still thinking of murdering me?"

"Because you kidnapped me and stranded me on a ship somewhere in the Atlantic, Smithton? It would be difficult. You took my weapons, remember?"

"My dear Captain, you are the most resourceful woman I know. You wouldn't let a little thing like lack of weapons stop you!"

"I am still contemplating it." She paused. "It's amazing, really, how often I think about killing you. What do you believe that says about your hopes for a successful marriage?"

"At least you are thinking about me. It's a start."

She gnawed her lip. "Julius will be worried about me."

"I left a note with Cooper telling Davies you decided to hoist anchor and sail off to England."

She snorted, inelegantly. "Do you think he'll believe that without hearing it from my own lips?"

Justin's mouth tightened and that small muscle began throbbing at his jaw.

"How Davies feels about your leaving is not my concern, Christine. The important thing is you are here by my side. Where you belong."

She yanked her arm out from his and put her hands on her hips, legs braced.

"By your side where I belong? Like a dog returned to her master? I think not, *milord*!" She turned on her heel and left him standing alone on deck.

Hellfire and damnation! Justin itched to yank his countess back and thrash that shapely behind receding into the distance. She was so prickly still, even the mildest conversation could turn her like a hawk ready to pounce on an unsuspecting and innocuous mouse.

Or rat, more like, he thought ruefully. Certainly that's how Chris would view him if he followed through on his impulse to paddle her. And she'd be right. He mentally kicked himself for forgetting his plans to woo his wife with honey, not vinegar. For someone who bragged on his own charming and winning ways, he certainly was making a hash of it now. A few weeks at sea and they'd either be reconciled, or one of them would be murdered.

He thought the latter more likely, with him in the victim's role.

Christine paced the cabin, back and forth, winding like a timepiece. Arrogant buggerin' sod! Just when she thought there was some hope for peace between them, he'd go and say something sure to light her fuse and set her off. Walking holes into the deck wasn't going to help her situation.

She rummaged through the small bureau and found blank foolscap and a pencil. Sitting on the bunk with the paper spread across the Marvell, she made two columns and lists. Against—Arrogant. Too pretty. Domineering and controlling. English aristo. Snores. For—Funny. Smart. Pretty. Emerald eyes. Silky black hair. Hard, shapely body. Makes me laugh. Dances with me.

I love him.

There was a sharp *crack* and Christine looked down. The pencil sat in two pieces in her hand. She was finally forced to acknowledge what she'd been feeling since she'd walked into Ganymede's Cup and seen her husband across the room. Maybe what she'd been feeling since that impulsive decision to take him aboard the *Tigress.*

I love him. God help me, I love him and I'm terrified.

She was still staring at the paper when there was a knock.

"Yes?"

"It's Thomas, ma'am. His lordship wanted me to let you know supper will be served in a couple hours and if you need anything pressed to wear that I should do it for you, if it please you."

Christine smiled at this earnest speech and opened the hatch. "I didn't know you'd been pressed into service as an abigail, young Thomas. Please, come in."

She stood aside and the sailor entered the cabin clutching his hat, cheeks aflame at her gentle roasting. She took pity on him and asked him to wait a moment while she rummaged through the locker. There in the trunk, neatly folded, was a red silk crepe evening dress.

"Oh my," Thomas breathed, blushing as scarlet as the gown.

"Indeed," she mused. "Let me see if there is something more subdued in here."

The only other evening gown was one of forest green velvet, suitable for England, too warm for the tropical waters.

"Red it is, Thomas. It only needs a touch up to be ready this evening."

"Oh, mum, I'll handle it as if it were the captain's own!" he promised.

"Merciful Heavens, Thomas, Captain Jackson would look a sight in this gown!"

That got a chuckle out of the boy and a promise to have it back in plenty of time. Cheered by her conversation, Christine rummaged a bit more, finding a satin bandeau to match the gown, a shawl of rich-hued paisley silk, and even a pair of kid slippers. They were a bit tight, especially after the comfort of men's footgear for so many months, but she stoutly told herself if she could suffer through bound breasts and convenient gourds, she could handle a light corset and pinching slippers.

Her glance fell on the list on the bunk. It was early in the voyage yet. Much could happen before the ship docked.

Thomas returned with the gown and she assured him it was "'shipshape and Bristol fashion', as you English would say." She pressed a coin into his hand and reminded him to return the men's clothing to her in the morning. After he stumbled out of the cabin, still blushing, she stripped down to her chemise and found a "divorce corset"—a device requiring no back lacing—in the bottom of the trunk.

She grinned at the thought of Justin purchasing a garment with such negative overtones. Christine eased the dress over her head and pulled up the long sleeves. The neckline dipped low, but not shockingly so. Blonde lace draped the gown in an overskirt and trimmed the sleeves. She ran a hand down the smooth fabric. It seemed like forever since she'd worn a gown, and she'd never worn one this stunningly sophisticated.

"I had it made for you in St. Augustine."

She whirled, clutching the unfastened gown to her bosom. Justin leaned against the hatchway, arms crossed, watching her with hooded eyes.

"When I thought of you wearing it, I imagined you would look like a column of flame. Not every woman can wear that color. But I knew you could."

He ducked his head and entered. She backed up a step. The cabin seemed much, much smaller. A lock of his dark hair had fallen across his forehead and she almost reached out to brush it back with her hand when he stopped, close to her.

"As you've no doubt guessed, Christine, this is my cabin. I hoped to convince you to accompany me back to the *Griffin* of your own will, and I had the cabin readied with that in mind. I hope you find it comfortable." He took a deep breath and braced himself, as if preparing for a blow. "I didn't plan on kidnapping you. I won't lie to you," he added softly. "I don't know how far I would have gone to convince you. And I could not imagine sailing away without you. When you fell during the fight, it seemed like a sign, and I still believe bringing you here was the right thing to do."

Her eyes narrowed. "I'm supposed to believe that story, when there is a trunk full of women's clothing here?"

Justin smiled ruefully. "I was taking a chance. I believed I could convince you to come with me and I didn't like the idea of having to borrow clothes from the sailors to keep you covered across the Atlantic."

"Knowing you as I do, Smithton, I find it difficult to believe you would have allowed me to simply walk out of the tavern and let you sail away."

"I have learned, Christine, that fate sometimes conspires to alter our best laid plans. As you know, opportunities arise, and the prudent person seizes them."

He turned to leave. She stopped him with a hand on his arm and a sigh.

"Don't go. This has all happened at once and I have much to think about." She smiled wanly. "And I'm willing to admit I desperately need your assistance at the moment or I will have to call Thomas back. Please."

Justin looked into her eyes and she desperately wished she could better read the expression there. Whatever he was feeling for her at that moment—for good or for bad—he was keeping it on a tight rein.

"Turn around."

Christine turned. He began fastening the loops marching down her back, pausing after the fourth one. Her nerves were on edge and, right when she was about to snap at him, she felt the whisper brush of his fingers where her neck sloped into her shoulder. A gentle touch, moving to stroke the small curls at the nape of her neck.

Very well, now she had an inkling of what he was feeling about her, at least at this moment, and her nerves were brought to the edge. It was too soon. She could not control herself when he touched her like that.

"Your skin is so soft." His voice was low, sending a slight tremor through her. She started to turn and he put gentle hands on her shoulders. "Shh...I want to remember."

He resumed slowly fastening her dress. "There was a large tree growing outside the guesthouse at your home in St. Augustine."

"A magnolia," she said huskily.

The long fingers paused, resting on the warm skin below her shoulders. "It had white flowers," he continued, fastening up the gown. "I plucked one and the petals were lush. Full of life. Soft. But not as soft as this."

He leaned forward and she felt his lips brush the base of her neck where his fingers had been a moment before. She could feel the heat of his body behind her and it was all she could do not to lean back into that warmth and solidity.

"Raise the curls off your neck, Christine."

She reached behind her and pulled the gilded curls up and away. Her hair was still too short to pin up, but a good brushing had restored its shine and the bandeau from the trunk put it in order with curls around her face for a softer look. She thought he'd wanted to fasten the last loop, but suddenly there was something cool and heavy around her neck. She glanced into the shaving mirror on the bulkhead and saw a double strand of matched pearls resting on her bosom. Justin was watching her over her shoulder in the mirror.

"I know by that look on your face, you are going to say something foolish, Christine. Do not. For months I have been thinking of how you'd look, right at this moment, gowned in crimson with pearls shimmering at your throat. Allow me my small pleasure to look my fill."

He adjusted the clasp and turning her around, stepped back, giving her a long, slow perusal from slippers to hair. Then he smiled broadly.

"I am the most fortunate of husbands," he said simply, and extended his arm to escort her to dinner.

Smithton led his countess in to the captain's cabin, the scarlet gown a startling contrast to the more soberly clad merchant seamen.

"I say, your ladyship," said Ridley, the purser, "that's a smashing rig!"

"Belay that, mister!" grumbled Captain Jackson as Christine gave the young man a smile. Ridley smiled back until he saw the earl glaring at him, then he decided to examine his silverware.

Over supper they discussed affairs between Britain and the new American states, beginning to resume normal trade now that the war was over between the mother country and its wayward child.

"And now that they're done tangling with us, I hope the Yankees can put that navy of theirs to work blasting the pirates from these waters, damn their eyes!"

Christine wasn't sure if the last was for the Americans or the pirates, but graciously accepted the captain's hastily offered apology.

Jackson continued with his tirade. "I hear the United States is sending someone to clean out those rascals in the Keys. I wish him luck because he's going to need it."

Ridley chortled. "The United States is barely a country! What can they do that the Spaniards and British haven't been able to do against the pirates?"

Christine raised her glass of claret, examined the color in the lamplight, then gave the young officer a small, tight smile. "Talk in St. Augustine, Mr. Ridley, is that Mr. Monroe is going to send Captain David Porter to the Keys. If I were a wagering person, I'd bet on Porter and not the pirates."

The older seamen at the table nodded. Too many of them had had encounters with the American navy's frigates and their captains during the late war to dismiss them out of hand, and Porter's *Essex* had been a particularly lethal foe.

Jackson deftly steered the conversation away from American naval victories. "Piracy is a serious problem, milady. Not far back, the *Maria Louisa* was attacked off the Florida Keys and the crew and passengers were lucky to escape with their lives."

"Why, Lord Smithton's own ships have been attacked by pirates and he was held for ransom!" Ridley said, outraged.

"Justin, you never told me!" Christine turned in her seat, so only her husband could see the laughter lurking in her dark eyes. "Did you lose much?"

His own gaze was sober as he looked into her face.

"I survived relatively unscathed," he said. "I did lose something valuable to me, but I have confidence the new owner will treasure it and keep it well."

"That Christopher Daniels is the worst of the lot!" Ridley said emphatically, bringing Christine's attention back before she could puzzle out Justin's statement.

"Have you ever, uh, met Captain Daniels?"

"No, but I've heard tales of him from others in Delerue Shipping! An arrogant young fop who surrounds himself with the most degenerate scum of the Florida coast! If we were ever to meet up with him, we'd show him a thing or two!"

"Would you now?" Christine purred, opening her fan and fluttering it to move the humid air. "I feel ever so much safer, Mister Ridley, knowing *Sanders*-Delerue is in such capable hands."

She winced behind her fan as her husband kicked her ankle under the table even as he solicitously poured her more wine. She moved her ankle out of harm's way and studied the relaxed relationship between Justin and Captain Jackson.

"Have you two known each other long?"

Jackson grinned. "I had this sprat under my command when he first shipped out for Delerue. His father wanted him to get his sea legs and learn where the gold came from that paid for the fine house and clothes young lordlings wear."

"And what kind of a sailor was he?"

"Green, milady, and I mean that in every sense of the word! He spent the first three days with his head over a bucket, but after that he found his bearings and came around."

Justin bore the ribbing good-naturedly, a small smile on his mouth as he swirled the wine in his glass. "It's a wonder you didn't toss me overboard, Jackson. Heaven knows I gave you enough cause."

"You earned your keep soon enough. I knew after a time you'd be an asset to your father's business. I never expected you to inherit the title, though. I always thought you'd be making the Florida run with me."

Justin sighed. "That was the plan, and all I ever wanted. To be aboard ship, traveling to new places, meeting new people. But after poor Roger broke his neck riding..." He shrugged. "You do what you have to do, not always what you want to do."

Christine stared at him. How selfish she'd been not to think Justin too might have had dreams and plans thrown into upheaval. She never thought about how he might miss and mourn his older brother, and what it cost him to inherit the title. To her, he'd always been the earl.

She knew all too well what it meant to be told your future wasn't your own, that your place was predetermined and set. She sat quietly, sipping her wine and thinking.

After supper, Justin invited her to take a stroll around the deck while he smoked. She looped her arm through his, enjoying the peacefulness of being with him, not wrangling again.

"Justin?"

"Hmmm?"

"Last night at the tavern. You were trying to tell me something…something important." Her brow furrowed. "I really wish I could remember what it was!"

He stood silent for a moment, smoking, the cheroot's small coal gleaming in the dark.

"Give yourself time, Christine. You took quite a blow to the head."

She cocked her head and tried to make out his features in the dark, but all she could see was his shadowed outline and the red coal.

"If I don't remember, will you tell me again?"

He moved closer and clasped her hand where it rested atop his arm.

"Yes, Christine. If you don't remember on your own, I'll tell you again what I said last night at the tavern."

She didn't know why this made her feel relieved, but she accepted his explanation as they finished their stroll. He escorted her back to their cabin and she swallowed as he entered after her, securely closing the hatch.

"Are you spending the night here, Justin?"

He raised his eyebrows, then smiled, his eyes crinkling at the corners. "I do believe that's my gear stowed in that trunk, Christine. Why, this must be my cabin!"

"Very droll, Smithton," she muttered. "All I meant was, it will be, well, *awkward* sharing a cabin. At night."

He chuckled and began untying his cravat, humming under his breath. "Don't worry, my dear Captain. Even though we do have to share the bunk, and it does look like it'll be a rather snug fit, I promise to control myself. After all," he said loftily, "not all of us are ravening, lust-maddened pirates."

She stonily ignored him and began to remove her own clothes, again frustrated by the fastenings of her evening dress.

"Tsk. Stop that before you tear it." He walked across the cabin and turned her around. He undid the gown, not lingering as he had when fastening it up. He helped her with the clasp of the pearls, as impersonally efficient as any lady's maid, then ignored her as she washed, hurriedly pulled a night rail over her head and made use of the cabin's private facilities.

Christine came out from the head and stopped dead in the cabin's center.

Justin was stretched on the bunk, the covers low around his hips. Everything else was bare. His bronzed shoulders gleamed in the lamplight, the hair on his chest arrowed to a point somewhere below the covers, the muscles of his chest flexing with his breath. But what held her attention fast was the paper in his hand.

He was reading her list.

"Give me that!" she hissed, dashing across the cabin. When she got to the bunk and made a grab for the paper, he lashed one arm around her and flipped her face down across the bunk, his body atop hers and pinning her in place.

"Get off of me, you oaf!"

"Shhh—I'm trying to read here."

She reached behind her, clawing, and connected with naked flesh. He yelped and grabbed her hand, holding it at the base of her back. She huffed impotently and tried to buck him off.

"Dammit, your knee is digging into my hip!"

"That isn't my knee. Hellfire, I think I'm bleeding where you scratched me, wench! Now hold still. Let's see here... 'Against—arrogant. Too pretty. Domineering and controlling. English aristo.' So far I don't see any faults here, Christine."

She snarled an obscenity into the covers and squirmed again. He caught his breath and put his mouth very close to her ear.

"Keep that up, my dear, and I'll never finish reading this list."

She froze.

"'Snores?' I do not snore, madam! 'For—Funny. Smart. Pretty.' Do you really think I am pretty, Christine?" He finished reading in blessed silence.

She jumped when she felt the puff of air next to her ear. "'Hard, shapely body'? You're putting me to the blush here, love."

"Hardheaded!" She whispered back fiercely. "You are a hardheaded idiot!"

His lips rested just below her earlobe and she felt them draw back in a smile. "If you're sure that's what you meant."

He finally released her hand and shifted his body off of hers. He leaned up and blew out the lantern, then settled back down, still keeping one arm around her middle and holding her back against him, spoon fashion.

Christine pulled up the covers, pointedly ignoring him. The bunk was reasonably sized for one, but, as he'd pointed out, snug when two people occupied it. She had the choice of either sleeping with her nose jammed against the bulkhead or easing into her naked husband's embrace.

She scooted carefully against him. He was still awake. Very much awake, throbbing against her backside. She wondered how she'd ever sleep over the weeks ahead when she felt the lightest brush across her night rail. She glanced down from beneath her lashes. Justin's hand lay loosely cupped where it rested below her breast, then there it was again, the sweep of his long, thick thumb against her nipple. Her flesh strained against the lawn fabric and she'd swear it swelled even as she watched, trying to bring itself into contact with that thumb again.

"Smithton, stop that."

"Mmmm?"

"You know what I'm talking about. Move your hand!"

"Well, if you insist..." His entire hand engulfed her breast, rolling her nipple between thumb and forefinger. "Is that better?"

Oh, yes, that was *so* much better. She sternly told herself she needed to get out of the bunk and sleep in the chair, but when she told her legs to move, the only movement she seemed capable of producing was to arch her back into his hand for more. He obliged by lightly squeezing and, at her muffled moan, repeated the motion before moving to give her other, neglected breast his attention. She only had a moment to wonder where his other hand was before she felt it, clutching handfuls of fabric and pulling it up and over her hip.

All the reasonable little voices in her head telling her this was a bad idea were overruled by the throb low in her belly and another voice from a primitive part of her brain whispering, *It's been six months, dammit!* Her mind was further muddled by a tongue licking its way across her neck and down her shoulder, pausing to place soft kisses on the bullet scar before moving back up and around her ear.

"Raise your hips, love."

She blindly obeyed. He pulled her night rail up and off, and ripped it lengthwise, the sound startlingly loud in the small cabin.

"Wha—"

Before she could question further, he'd flipped her onto her back and held both hands over her head, wrapping the cloth around her wrists. It wasn't tight, but when she pulled, she couldn't free them. She stared at him. His face was intent, grim, the planes etched with shadows in the soft light.

"Untie me!"

He ignored her command as he tore the remaining cloth into two segments and, sitting astride her kicking legs, secured first one foot, then the other to the bottom of the bunk. She managed to pull her hands back to hit him, but with her hands tied and on her back, she couldn't do serious damage, especially when he grabbed her bound wrists and pulled them above her head, slipping the cloth over the lantern hook at the head of the bunk.

She was now bound hand and foot, not painfully, but feeling uncomfortably aware of her exposure and vulnerability. Justin rocked back on his heels, unselfconscious in his own nakedness, surveying his handiwork with grim satisfaction.

She glared at him.

"Do you know what your problem is, Christine?"

"That I haven't killed you yet and saved myself this aggravation?"

"Tut-tut." He chucked her under the chin. "Don't make me gag you as well. No, my dear, your problem is you think too much. And you are afraid."

"I am not afraid of you!" she hissed, pulling futilely at the ties.

"I didn't say you were afraid of me," he said in a low voice. "I'll tell you what you are afraid of. You are afraid of losing control. You're afraid of putting yourself in someone else's hands."

He accompanied this by stroking his hands down her arms. She stifled a small cry at the sensation, ticklish and raw. He ignored the interruption and continued to smooth his hands along her body.

"There is something about being tied, Christine—and I know what I am talking about—helpless and dependent. It makes you focus on the other person in the room."

He continued to address her in dry tones accompanied by light strokes and pats along her body. She squirmed, having trouble concentrating, but he was still talking.

"Take us, for instance. We are going to be together for a few weeks, maybe longer, and I have to trust you not to slit my throat while I sleep. And I do trust you. But you sit here, making lists, because you are not willing to let yourself believe what you feel is acceptable. You are afraid to trust and to take a chance."

His hand was stroking along her throat, delicately tickling behind her ear. She turned her head, but he put his hand along her jaw and brought it back.

"Pay attention, my dear, this is an important lesson."

His hooded eyes never left hers as his hand slid down her sweat-dewed chest and rested against her breast, his fingers making small circles around her nipple. She tried not to respond and licked lips gone dry while he talked on.

"Tonight, you have to trust me, Christine. Your body is open, vulnerable. You could scream. However, I can assure you no one would help you, for you are my wife and I am not just your husband, but the owner of this ship. They won't interfere with us. Do you believe me?"

She nodded, wary.

"You can't even leave this cabin. Right now, I could inflict a great deal of pain." The fingers resting against her nipple tightened, until the pressure brought a gasp from her throat, and then relaxed, stroking softly again. "And there's nothing you could do about it. But I don't want you to feel pain. I want you to feel pleasure. I want you to feel the freedom that comes from giving control to another, from trusting."

He punctuated this last by leaning forward and taking her earlobe between his teeth, nipping lightly. "Trust me, Christine."

Trust him? If she admitted she trusted him, it would be tantamount to admitting she cared for him far more deeply than he knew. She wanted to tell him that she knew he wouldn't hurt her body, but she still couldn't be sure he wouldn't hurt her heart. She *was* afraid of him, though she'd never admit to such. Afraid that when they were settled in England he'd be disappointed in her, sorry he'd brought her back. Being Justin, he'd try to never let it show, but she'd know nonetheless.

For now, it was all she could do not to cry out as he continued his attentions to her bound body. Her breath came in short, shallow pants as he moved down her belly, light kisses outlining her ribs, along her thighs, moving closer, ever closer to where she ached for more than kisses.

He raised his head and looked at her, dark eyes glittering in the shadows.

"You are holding back, Christine, fighting what you feel. Let go and trust your husband."

"I can't!" she gasped.

He smiled, a predator's gleam in the dark.

"You can and you will yield all."

He bent his head and put his mouth on her. She yelped and jerked, her bonds holding her in place. He ignored her frantic struggles and suddenly she wasn't fighting him any more. Sensations were roiling through her, spreading out in waves like ripples from a water-tossed stone.

"That's it, let go now, sweetheart. You taste like the ocean, warm and full of life. And here," he murmured, "a pearl."

He punctuated with a graze of his sharp teeth and soothed a moment later with his tongue, falling into a rhythm that had her moaning encouragement. She felt the ripples beginning in her body and he responded, thrusting two fingers inside her while suckling hard.

Her world shattered into a thousand multicolored fragments of fire. Her body rose off the bunk and for a moment, the tension held her until her shuddering ceased and she collapsed back, barely aware as her husband moved atop of her.

"Open your eyes," he commanded.

It took all her remaining energy, but she dragged her eyelids open, her breath still coming shallow and fast. He hovered above her, his own need stark in the planes of his face, the sweat streaking his jaw.

"Say it!" he demanded hoarsely.

She licked dry lips and knew no quarter would be offered. Sherry brown eyes met green in the dim cabin and she gave what she could.

"I trust you, Justin. And I yield—in this!"

He smiled crookedly. "A fighter to the bitter end."

He leaned down and kissed her and she tasted herself on his lips. He reached up and undid the loops securing her hands and then her feet, freeing her before bracing his hands alongside her head.

"Now, we'll take this journey together."

He took her hard and fast as she wrapped her long legs around his waist, pulling her to a place where she stopped thinking and shared the passion and the trust and other, stronger feelings she wouldn't think about. Thinking would come later.

For now there was only this, the two of them together, moving in a dance older than time, slick bodies sliding against one another, the friction and tightness building and clenching, her nails digging into his back as he muttered encouragement in her ear, dark words that took her even higher.

When the wave crested and broke, it rolled them both, together, and as they eased down she again opened her eyes to see Justin gazing into her face.

"I want to remember you like this, always, Christine. I will not betray your trust, I swear it."

He kissed her softly, then kept her in the circle of his arms through the night, a captive to his heart.

Chapter 16

Christine was alone in the morning. She winced as she climbed out of the bunk, smiling to herself at the unexpected stiffness in her limbs, the aching in muscles long unused. Justin had woken her again before dawn by licking his way down her back, outlining each vertebra and whispering in detail all the things he was going to do to her. She'd sleepily threatened to do something piratical and nasty to *him* if he didn't stop talking and get on with it, a command he'd obeyed with alacrity and skill.

She finished dressing before Thomas appeared with fresh water and breakfast, including rolls that he assured her were hardly stale at all, yet.

"If you put enough jam on it, it's quite tasty, milady," he said helpfully.

She solemnly thanked him for his assistance and promised to use plenty of jam. Of course Thomas blushed, and shyly added, "You look pretty today, ma'am."

She smiled and thanked him again. The chintz dress she wore was in the newer style, with the waistline dropped to a lower point than in her old gowns. This one featured a bodice of dark green above a white, flounced skirt. The sleeves had an Elizabethan look, with slashings of gold, and a gold waistband, a color echoed in the collar. The entire ensemble was fresh-looking and brought out the amber depths of her eyes.

Not much good for climbing the rigging, but fine feathers just the same. She looked at herself in the glass. It was a costume of a different sort than "Captain Daniels," but a costume nonetheless. This one was the "Countess" costume that, when donned, meant she was to play yet another role.

So which costume is the real Christine? she mused. Suddenly she grinned at the thought of her old, hollow gourd and how it would look if Lady Smithton hoisted her frothy skirts and stood at the rail with the sailors. The earl would *not* approve!

She tied her bonnet beneath her chin and, still grinning, went abovedeck to join her husband. Justin was sitting beneath a canvas awning, examining some papers. He looked up and smiled when he heard his wife approach, and stood, inviting her to join him.

"You look lovely in that gown, Christine. Charming as a summer day."

She glanced down at her half boots, then up at him from under her lashes. "I haven't thanked you yet for these lovely clothes. I appreciate the trouble you went to on my behalf."

"It was my pleasure, though it would be better if you thank Suzanne. She was the one who pored over the books with the modistes in St. Augustine and Savannah and picked out the materials. I only supplied the measurements."

Christine arched her brows as she took the seat alongside him.

"You have an amazing memory, Smithton. These clothes are a good fit."

His glance was warm as it traveled over her from head to toes.

"We had your old dresses and footgear to measure from and I only had to dredge up images of our past meetings to make the adjustments. And recalling those meetings was a pleasure, I assure you."

Over the rest of the morning, they talked. He showed her the records of his shipments from Florida. They discussed how business might be affected by the United States taking over Spain's possession, and whether there was any future in silkworm farming. Christine was so caught in learning the ropes of his ventures that she was startled by the call from aloft.

"Sail ho!"

The sailor was pointing to the ship's stern and another vessel coming up on them.

"Is it the *Tigress*?" Justin asked her as she scanned the water.

"No, that's not her rigging."

They moved alongside Captain Jackson. Jackson was watching the vessel through his telescope, his experienced eye judging the distance and speed at which the ship was gaining on the *Griffin*. And it was gaining on them. He tugged thoughtfully at his side whiskers, then turned to the earl and countess, putting a reassuring smile on his face.

"It's probably nothing, sir, but I like to be cautious, especially when I have passengers aboard. Perhaps you'd like to go below, m'lady."

Christine's hand was up, shading her eyes. "Give me your glass, Captain."

He raised bushy brows at her peremptory tone, but handed the telescope over. She focused on the ship. Something about her lines was familiar…"Havana," she muttered, thinking back to the Cuban port.

An image rose in her mind of a Spaniard reeking of cheap cologne.

"Bloody hell." She focused for a better view. "Those are pirates, Captain!"

Captain Jackson chuckled indulgently. "My dear Countess," he lied, trying to soothe her, "there are no pirates around here."

"Oh yes?" Christine glared at him. "And I suppose Captain Christopher Daniels is just a figment of everyone's imaginations?"

"I'm fairly certain that is not Captain Daniels," Justin pointed out.

"I know that, that's Ramon Ramirez's ship! They're the ones who took the *Maria Louisa!* He's only one scurvy rat, but rats bite!" She put her hand on his arm. "Please, Justin, tell them to prepare for battle."

Justin saw the trust in his wife's eyes, and put his hand over hers. "Am I not an indulgent husband?" he said softly, then louder, "You heard her ladyship, Jackson. You are in command of this vessel. However, my wife has an…instinct about these matters. I believe it comes from the time when she was in charge of Sanders Shipping with her father."

Jackson looked at her sharply. "You're Daniel Sanders's daughter?"

She nodded.

Jackson stroked his side-whiskers and assessed the young countess. "Well, my lady, you may indeed have an instinct for smelling pirates. Your father was a knowing one. I suppose you know that rogue Julius Davies as well?"

"I was practically raised by Julius after my mother died. We are still close," she added, ignoring Justin's impolite snort.

"Hmm—well, whoever that Spanish ship is, she seems in an awful hurry to catch up to us. Mr. Ridley," he called, "break out the weapons and have the men stand to and prepare for action."

Christine took Justin's hand. "Thank you."

"For what?"

"For believing me. For acknowledging me in front of Jackson and not dismissing my advice."

Justin raised her hand to his lips. "I would be foolish to dismiss your concerns. This is, after all, an area of expertise for you, as I've learned to the regret of my own fortunes."

She surprised herself by blushing. Then she frowned. "Have you ever…" She cleared her throat, which had suddenly become husky. "Have you fought at sea, Justin?"

"You mean other than my ill-fated meeting with the *Tigress*? Never fear. Jackson is an old hand at fending off invaders and, when I sailed with him, I had my share of action. Why don't you go below, Chr—"

"Good idea!" she interrupted him and he frowned, not expecting acquiescence. She headed for the hatch as the familiar sound of men's voices raised in the excitement of preparation for battle swirled about. Justin grabbed her arm and swung her around.

"For luck," he murmured, and bent her slender back over his arm as he brought his mouth down on hers. Christine's lips parted beneath her husband's and without hesitation she brought her arms around his neck, holding him closer and molding his form to hers as if to imprint it on her very soul. Reluctantly, he finally released her and watched as she paused in the hatchway, glancing at him again before disappearing below.

The ship bearing down was a schooner, smaller but faster than the *Griffin* laden with timber, rice, sugar, and indigo for its voyage home. The pursuing ship, now identified by the markings on its side as the *Santiago,* didn't pretend to be anything but a predator. It carried seven guns including a pivot mount, and could do substantial damage to a lone merchantman.

Jackson pulled at his whiskers. If they were captured, the best fate the earl and countess could hope for would be ransom. He didn't dwell on other possibilities, but the *Griffin* wasn't totally defenseless and included veteran sailors of England's fight against Napoleon. They'd faced heavy fire before and he took comfort in the efficient preparations of his seasoned crew.

Justin returned armed with a heavy, lethal-looking blade, while the captain checked the priming on a brace of pistols. They were joined by a slender young man carrying a sword and sliding a pistol into the belt at his waist. Jackson glanced at him, then looked again, recognizing the countess. He gave a small grunt of approval. Apparently the woman had more wit than hair after all. If she had to defend herself, and from the way she handled her blade she knew what she was about, it was better done in breeches than petticoats.

Justin took in Christine's outfit and sighed.

"I thought I had seen the last of those clothes when you gave them to Thomas."

"Don't blame him. I insisted on getting them back. And he loaned me his best cap. Good thing I held onto these garments. Hard to swing a blade in a dress. Those tight sleeves will do you in." She smiled at him, feeling the familiar exhilaration she'd come to anticipate before a battle. Everything seemed sharper—all her senses heightened.

"What are you grinning at, Christine?"

"I was thinking that, so far, being married to you has been anything but dull."

"Odd. That is exactly what I was thinking."

Captain Jackson was bringing the *Griffin* about and hauling in sail. He hoped an aggressive and prepared stance might send the *Santiago* away to search for easier prey.

"Captain, they're hailing us!" called Ridley. They could make out individuals on the pirate ship by now and there was a pockmarked man in a wide-brimmed Spanish hat glaring at them. Next to him stood a one-armed ruffian with a horn.

"Ahoy the *Griffin*!" called the one-armed man. "You're outgunned and outmanned! Surrender your ship now and we won't harm you. Resist and we'll blast you to the bottom!"

"I am tired of being threatened by pirates," Justin said. Christine, wisely, said nothing.

Jackson nodded to Ridley who gave the order to fire the *Griffin's* starboard guns. The first blast took away some rigging and started a small fire that was quickly brought under control, and the *Santiago* moved in for boarding.

Justin yanked Christine behind him as a blast from the pirates' guns rocked the merchantman and sent splinters flying. She wrenched herself out of his arms.

"Dammit, let go of me! Neither one of us will be any good to Captain Jackson if you don't let me alone."

She gripped his upper arms, her face grim. "Trust *me*, Justin! I know what I'm about here."

She could see his desire to protect her warring with the logic of her statements. Whatever he wanted to say, though, was lost as the *Griffin* rocked under another assault. The pirates were within boarding range and time had run out.

Justin kissed her hard, said, "Stay here then, but be careful, dammit!" Then he thrust her away to join Jackson. She was close behind him until a balding pirate bore down on her, cutlass raised high. She brought her own blade up to the ready, twisting to escape his blow. He grinned at her through the black stubs of his teeth, using his strength to beat her back, but she kept up her guard, looking for a way to slip in. It came when he drew back for a killing backslash and her blade slipped between his ribs. She twisted her wrist and pulled her sword free in time to block the downward stroke, catching his blade close to her hilt.

The slimmer sword snapped, but it wasn't needed now. It had done its task and the pirate fell facedown, his last expression one of puzzlement.

She threw the shattered sword aside, bile rising in her throat. Stabbing into living flesh wasn't the same as hitting a wooden target. She had no time to dwell on it as she grabbed her fallen foe's weapon. The blood-streaked hilt was slippery and she gripped it tight in her gloved hand.

"Look out, m'lady!"

She ducked and brought the cutlass around to deflect a blow from behind, the strength of the attack jarring her arm and pushing her to her knees. She grabbed her dirk in her left hand and slashed upward from below, opening her assailant's inner thigh. He screamed and clutched at the spouting wound, but she was already turning toward her rescuer.

Young Thomas had his back against a barrel, dirk in hand. A pirate was bearing down on him, his reach and weapon giving him ample advantage over the lad.

"Turn around, pig, and face someone your own size!"

The pirate was distracted for a moment and did turn, giving Thomas opportunity to duck beneath his arm. Rather than run, the lad clambered up on the barrel and grabbing a belaying pin, smashed it alongside the pirate's head, dropping him like a felled pine.

Christine blew out her breath in a rush. "Thank you, Thomas. You're a good man in a fight!"

"As are you, m'lady! I mean...I'm sorry..." he stammered.

She winked. "I told you I needed these clothes!" Distracted, she looked beyond the boy and saw the tide of battle turning and the pirates trying to slip back to their ship. She spotted Ramirez inching toward the rail.

"Halt, Ramirez, you won't escape this time!"

Ramirez looked up, startled at being addressed by name, and then his small eyes narrowed on his opponent.

"*Hijo de puta*! Daniels! I remember you!" the pirate hissed. "You think you can take me on? Without your big friend Davies to protect you?"

Chris started forward when a hand shot out and clamped her wrist.

"Oh, please," Justin drawled, "this once let me play the man. It would mean so much to me."

Smithton's fine coat was gone and blood and dirt smeared his shirt, but he didn't appear injured. Christine grinned and saluted with the bloody blade, stepping back as Justin faced the pirate.

"He's all yours, milord."

Ramirez sneered. "I see Daniels has a new lover. Let us see if he still wants you when your face is slashed away!"

Justin said nothing but brought his blade up, and the two men circled one another. Even though her husband had more bulk and reach, Christine's hand clenched tight around her hilt. Ramirez lived with his blade and Justin was a merchant, not a warrior.

Justin locked eyes with his foe, their blades tapping lightly as each began the dance of feint and parry, looking for an opponent's weakness. Both were hampered by the smoke and slippery deck. Justin balanced lightly on his feet, body turned to present the slimmest target.

Ramirez was grinning, but his face was covered with oily sweat, and his eyes flickered nervously to his crew scrambling over the side. At that moment, Justin lunged, fully engaging him.

Christine relaxed fractionally. Her husband was in control of the situation, driving Ramirez back and putting him on the defensive.

Justin felt the shift in the fighting and knew the tide had turned in their favor. He attacked with renewed vigor, driving Ramirez to the rail. Watching the pirate's eyes darting about, looking for a safe exit, Justin never saw the puddle of grease on the deck near the guns, and he slipped and had to grab the gun carriage with his left hand for support. He was able to block the first slash from Ramirez, but he knew there was no blocking the triumphant pirate's fatal downward thrust.

"Die, *maricón*!" Ramirez snarled, bringing the blade back for the killing blow.

A single shot rang out. For a moment, Ramirez hovered, a stunned expression on his face, before crumpling to the deck, blood oozing from a hole in his chest.

Justin rolled to his side to avoid the pirate falling on him and saw Christine lowering a smoking pistol.

"Thank you, my dear, for saving my life."

She looked at him blankly for a moment, then slid to the deck, landing hard on her backside as her legs gave out.

Justin sighed, called a sailor to see to the unconscious pirate, and pushed himself to his feet. He dipped some rum from the ration barrel and brought it to his wife, sitting on the deck with her head between her knees. He knelt beside her.

"Here, drink."

She took the cup in a trembling hand, rinsed her mouth and spat to the side. Then she took a swallow of the rum and passed the cup back to Justin, who took his time getting his own drink. He watched Jackson's crew rounding up the remaining pirates. They'd quickly thrown themselves on the *Griffin*'s mercy once Ramirez was out of action.

"You saved my life back there. Why?"

She turned to him, brown eyes wide. One gold-streaked curl had tumbled down from under her cap and he absently tucked it behind her ear.

"Had you not fired that shot, you'd now be a widow. A very wealthy widow with everything you wanted—freedom, power, money, and a portion of Delerue-Sanders Shipping. It only would've taken a moment's hesitation. Why did you save me?"

She opened her mouth to speak, then closed it again. She frowned, and only stared at him as if memorizing his face.

He waited patiently. For this answer, he was willing to wait as long as she needed.

Finally, she cleared her throat.

"I couldn't let Ramirez run you through. I'd have stopped him even if you'd been some dog on the street."

"Thank you for the thought," he said dryly. "But I don't believe that, my dear Captain. Think about it—everything you wanted was within your grasp. It *is* what you want, is it not? All the power and money? I am the only thing blocking your possession of all your dreams."

"That's not true," she said in a whisper.

"What is not true? That money and freedom are what you want? You have told me so often enough." He paused. "Or are you now getting greedy and wanting more?"

"I couldn't let him kill you, Justin. Not now."

"Why not now?"

He was inexorable. She lost her defensive look and glared at him. His heart began to beat faster. This was the Christine he was used to sparring with.

"What has changed, Christine?"

She exploded to her feet and glared down at him.

"It's you, all right? I couldn't let him kill you because I love you, dammit. I want bloody all of it! I want Sanders, I want the money, and I want you! There, are you happy, you stupid buggerin' sod? Stop laughing!"

She kicked him in the thigh. Hard enough to make her point. Justin surged to his feet and grabbed her close before she could kick him again. She tried anyway, so he cut off her breath by clamping his mouth over hers. When he lifted his head he was pleased to see she looked more dazed than mutinous.

"My dearest Captain, I'm counting on you making me happy for the next fifty years or so. And, yes, you harpy, we will work together to build our fortunes. We will need all the money we can earn for the heirs to the Delerue-Sanders Shipping lines."

"Sanders-Delerue Shipping!"

"We will argue about it below."

"Wait a minute," she ordered, slapping both hands on his chest and pushing him back. "You've bullied me into telling you why I'll stay with you. How do you really feel about me?"

"I was trying to tell you in the tavern before you got your wits scrambled. I love you, Christine Sanders Delerue. You foolish girl, do you think I would have chased you across the ocean just because of my pride? I chased you down because I love you! And I want my money back! Ow! Don't kick me again!"

He pushed her against the rail and kissed her. Really, it seemed the most effective way to get her in a complaisant mood, and he rather enjoyed the method. His own glance was gentle when he broke off and looked down at her.

"Very well, I'll bare my soul to you, my dear Captain. I cannot imagine living without you anymore. My heart was stolen aboard the *Tigress*."

He ran his knuckles softly over her dirt-streaked cheek. "I have confidence you'll treasure it and keep it well." He grinned and couldn't resist adding, "Besides, I've grown rather accustomed to the notion of being ravished nightly by a naughty pirate."

The haunted look shadowed her eyes again and she lost her bravado. She leaned her head against his chest so she wouldn't have to look into his eyes, and her voice was hardly more than a whisper.

"Justin, I'm so scared. Not like I was when I saw you fighting, but I'm scared of England. What if I'm not a good countess? What if I embarrass you?"

A chuckle rumbled through his chest and he leaned down and kissed the top of her head.

"You are most certainly an original, and I'm sure we'll be a nine-days wonder for the ton until a new scandal comes along. I have every confidence in you, my dear. Anyone who can command a ship of reprobates, face down the scum of the seas, *and* make a profit is someone I want by my side."

"Agggh! I'm bleeding to death here! *Madre de Dio*s, get help for me!"

Ramirez had regained consciousness and one of the *Griffin*'s officers was roughly tying off his wound as Jackson came over to inspect their prisoner.

"That will hold you 'til trial, Ramirez! With luck, you'll live to swing as an example to other scum," Jackson said with satisfaction.

Ramirez lifted his head with arrogance and Christine had to admire him for showing spirit when he knew what fate awaited him. But then Ramirez raised a bloody hand and shakily pointed at Smithton and Christine embracing.

"I will hang? What of that one there, Captain? Both of them deserve to hang, for that's the notorious Captain Christopher Daniels and his paramour!"

The *Griffin*'s men gaped at Ramirez like he'd suddenly sprouted horns and spoken gibberish. Ridley broke the silence first, his laugh braying out.

"Milord Smithton and his wife? Pirates? Christopher Daniels? Your brain's been scrambled, man. That's her ladyship, Countess Smithton!"

Ramirez's head snapped around and his eyes widened as Christine sketched him a short bow, then pulled off her cap, sending the golden curls tumbling out.

"Sorry to disappoint you, Captain Ramirez, but I'm an ordinary lady on her wedding voyage."

"You're doing it a bit too brown, my dear," Smithton murmured in her ear, keeping an eye on Chandler Jackson. The veteran sea captain was pulling at his whiskers and studying the countess speculatively, then he gave Justin a slight nod as if to say "it's your problem, boy."

"But...but...that's Daniels, I tell you! It's a man!"

Ramirez was still yelling insults and curses as the *Griffin's* sailors hustled him back to his captured ship. Jackson strolled over to the earl, keeping an eye on the lady at his side.

"We need to get the *Santiago* back to the American authorities, milord. I'm concerned, though, we'll be shorthanded when we send a prize crew over."

"It may not be necessary to leave yourself shorthanded." Christine was shading her eyes and looking to the west. "Help may come from another quarter."

"Ship off the port bow, Cap'n!" the lookout called.

It *looked* like the *Tigress*, flying American colors and coming up fast. Christine grinned widely when she saw the name painted on the bow. The schooner was now *Bonny Anne,* even if the figurehead was still a jungle cat, and Julius Davies was on deck alongside Cooper and Robin. The latter began waving wildly when he spotted Christine.

"Ahoy the *Griffin*!"

A weary Jackson took up his glass once again and eyed the oncoming ship. He recognized Davies and turned his gaze to the countess, who looked as if butter wouldn't melt in her mouth.

"What do you want, *Bonny Anne*?" he returned the hail.

"Why, as I live and breathe, it's Chandler Jackson! Do you need assistance, *Griffin*?"

"If you're offering, we could use a hand securing this bunch from the *Santiago*, Davies. What brings you out here?"

"We'd like a word with Lady Smithton. Is she able to come aboard?"

Justin tensed beside his wife, but she stepped in front of him, her back to the schooner, and put her hands on his chest.

"Let me go. Julius won't hold me against my will, and this way he'll know I've found safe anchorage and I'm staying with you of my own volition."

Justin's hands came up to cover hers and he gazed long into her sherry-colored eyes. Then he leaned forward and placed a soft kiss on her lips.

"Hurry back."

Justin watched his wife being rowed to her ship. The crew of the *Bonny Anne* was lined upon deck, and Christine paused for a word with each of the men who'd served under Captain Daniels. Some of them were shaking their heads in disbelief that they'd been fooled by this slender woman, but none seemed upset.

Justin snorted. Why should they be upset? She'd made them each a lot of money.

Finally, she came to her three friends. Justin couldn't hear what she said, but her actions spoke for themselves. A blushing Robin received a kiss on the cheek, and Richard a cuff on the arm and a firm handshake. She took Davies aside for an intense conversation that ended in a fierce embrace.

The older man looked over her head at Justin, grinning widely. Justin relaxed a fraction. He hadn't realized how much he'd wanted the rough pirate's approval. A final kiss from Julius, and Christine was climbing down the side of the ship, coming back to him.

The *Bonny Anne*'s crew cheered as their Captain gaily waved good-bye from the longboat, accompanied by Cooper to make arrangements with the *Griffin* for securing the *Santiago* and bringing it back to Florida. Justin helped her aboard and held her tight, and he could have sworn Cooper almost smiled to see them together.

Afterward they stood, arm in arm at the rail until the *Bonny Anne* and the *Santiago* were only specks on the horizon. Christine sniffed and Justin silently pressed his handkerchief into her hand. She pretended not to use it to dab at her eyes.

"Will we ever return?"

"But of course, my dear. We'll want to keep track of our investments—yours, mine, and ours. By the by, what will happen to Captain Christopher Daniel's fortune?"

"Julius will hold it in trust in America for the daughters of Christine and Justin Delerue, and a portion is being set aside to establish a home for retired sailors."

"Staffed, no doubt, by handsome young men," he said dryly. He turned to his bride, removed the cap from her head, and let her golden curls fly in the sea breeze.

"And that's the last, I hope, of Captain Daniels as well."

He made to toss the cap over the rail, but Christine stopped him and with an enigmatic smile took the cap and tucked it inside her jacket.

"I believe I will hold on to this, Smithton. You never know what tomorrow will bring."

He put his fingers below her chin and tilted her face upward.

"My dear Captain, if there is one thing I have learned over the past year, it's while tomorrow may bring unexpected adventures, I will enjoy them more with you at my side."

And then, in full view of the crew of the *Griffin*, Earl Smithton kissed his pirate countess, sealing a partnership that would be profitable and prolific.

Epilogue

St. Augustine, Florida, 2004

The tour guide from the St. Augustine Historical Society was winding up her presentation on the old house.

"And this is the library loft Countess Smithton mentioned in her journals. On their trips back to the United States, the earl and countess always stayed in her family home, adding to the guest quarters to accommodate their numerous offspring. The Delerues no longer had Florida companies after the Civil War and sold their St. Augustine properties."

The tour guide smiled, lines bracketing her mouth.

"The home they founded, Sailor's Rest, is now a bed and breakfast on St. George Street, said to be haunted by the ghost of a large, grinning man with a shaved head. There are some who say the spirit is that of Captain Christopher Daniels, others say it's the ghost of Julius Davies. All we know is the ghost is most likely to show himself when the moon is full and the B & B is hosting handsome young tourists."

About the Author

Aspiring authors are told to "write what you know," but Darlene Marshall has to admit she's never been a pirate. However, Marshall is a semi-native of North Florida and loves Florida history and the area the locals call "the other Florida"—a land of rolling hills and giant cockroaches, fire ants, scorpions, lightning strikes, and frog-drowning rainstorms. Only the strong (and the air-conditioned) survive.

Marshall is an alumna of the University of Florida (Go Gators!) and is the retired owner of a rock radio station. She's been a reporter and editor in television, radio, and print, and has worked at a drug treatment center teaching education and prevention. She loves science fiction, fantasy, and romance, tries to attend the World SF Convention each year, and has been married for over twenty-five years to a wonderful man who dances, brings her roses every week, and can tie a cherry stem in a knot with his tongue. They have two children and a dachshund who thinks she's queen.

Pirate's Price is Marshall's first novel with LTDBooks. Two more historical romances—*Smuggler's Bride* and *Captain Sinister's Lady*—will also be published by LTDBooks in 2005. Darlene Marshall loves to hear from fans. Contact her via email: darlenemarshall@cox.net or visit her website www.darlenemarshall.com